Stand-in Wife

THE MANNING BRIDES, BOOK TWO

STAND-IN WIFE

DEBBIE MACOMBER

THORNDIKE
CHIVERS

This Large Print edition is published by Thorndike Press, Waterville, Maine, USA and by BBC Audiobooks Ltd, Bath, England.
Thorndike Press, a part of Gale, Cengage Learning.
Copyright © 1992 by Debbie Macomber.
The moral right of the author has been asserted.
The Manning Brides #2

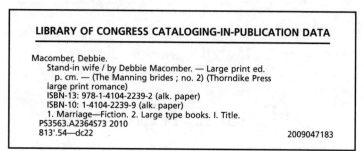

LIBRARY OF CONGRESS CATALOGING-IN-PUBLICATION DATA

Macomber, Debbie.
   Stand-in wife / by Debbie Macomber. — Large print ed.
     p. cm. — (The Manning brides ; no. 2) (Thorndike Press large print romance)
   ISBN-13: 978-1-4104-2239-2 (alk. paper)
   ISBN-10: 1-4104-2239-9 (alk. paper)
   1. Marriage—Fiction. 2. Large type books. I. Title.
PS3563.A2364S73 2010
813'.54—dc22   2009047183

BRITISH LIBRARY CATALOGUING-IN-PUBLICATION DATA AVAILABLE

Published in 2010 in the U.S. by arrangement with Harlequin Books S.A.
Published in 2010 in the U.K. by arrangement with Harlequin Enterprises II B.V.

U.K. Hardcover: 978 1 408 47834 9 (Chivers Large Print)
U.K. Softcover: 978 1 408 47835 6 (Camden Large Print)

Printed in the United States of America
1 2 3 4 5 6 7 14 13 12 11 10

To Lucy Beckstead

Thank you for showing me the way,
then taking me by the hand and guiding
me there

In Memory of Kim Gonzalez;
and for Tyler, who will never know his
mother

PROLOGUE

The morning was bleak, the sky, gray and overcast. The phone call from the hospital woke Paul Manning from a sound sleep — his first decent sleep since his daughter, Kelsey Diane, was born seventy-two hours earlier. Because of toxemia, his wife, Diane, had been placed in intensive care as a precaution.

Things quickly got worse, however, complicated by the fact that Diane had been born with only one kidney. Generally the toxins disappeared from the mother's body following birth, but in Diane's case that hadn't happened. Instead they'd attacked her liver and kidney, and before Paul fully realized the seriousness of her condition, she'd slipped into a coma. Paul and Diane's sister, Leah, had held a vigil at her side. After two days Dr. Charman had sent them home, promising to contact Paul if there was any change. Now he had.

"Could you come to the hospital?" he asked.

"What's wrong?" Paul demanded, frightened by the weariness in the physician's voice.

"It'd be best if you came to the hospital. I'll explain everything once you're here."

It wasn't supposed to happen like this.

A half hour later Paul Manning was shouting the words in his mind, but not a sound passed his lips. He was overwhelmed by pain, disbelief, shock — they punched him viciously, knocking the wind from his lungs. Dizzy and weak, he slumped into the hospital chair.

"We did everything we could," Dr. Charman murmured, his voice subdued with defeat.

Women gave birth . . . but they didn't die from it. Not in this day and age. Not when they were at one of the best medical facilities in the country.

The pregnancy had begun in a completely routine manner; Diane had never seemed healthier. Then, in the eighth month, she'd developed toxemia. Paul hadn't been too concerned, blithely unaware of how deadly her condition would prove to be.

Diane had suffered from toxemia during

her first pregnancy, too, and everything had turned out all right. The twins had been born six weeks premature, but the toxemia hadn't been life-threatening to either her or the boys.

"Is there someone you'd like me to call?"

Paul glanced up and shook his head. He didn't want his family just yet. For now he needed to grieve alone. "I'd like to be with her for a few minutes if I could."

Dr. Charman nodded and led the way down the quiet corridor to Diane's room. Paul's heart was pounding savagely, his head whirling, his legs unsteady. He felt as though he was in a nightmare, and he prayed someone would wake him up.

Dr. Charman opened the door and stepped aside. "I'll wait for you here," he said.

Paul nodded, surprised by the sudden calm that enveloped him. He hadn't expected to feel serenity. Not when the grief, the guilt and pain, were crushing his heart.

The first thing he noticed was that all the tubes had been disconnected. His wife's face glowed with a beauty that transcended anything he'd ever known. For a moment he was sure Dr. Charman had made a mistake, that Diane was only sleeping.

He remembered the first time he'd met

Diane six years earlier. He'd been in the army, stationed in Alaska, and she'd come up for the summer to work in a cannery. He was nearly thirty and she was barely twenty-one. Paul had taken one look at her, and it was as if his heart had stopped. He'd fallen in love a dozen times before, but no woman had ever affected him the way Diane Baker had. By the end of the summer, she'd decided to drop out of college and marry him.

They'd talked for hours on end, planning their future. Paul's degree was in journalism, but he intended to be a novelist one day. Diane read his work, built up his confidence, convinced him he'd sell his stories. Through the years her belief in him remained unwavering.

Six months after they were married she was pregnant. When she had Ryan and Ronnie, Paul thought his heart would burst with pride. He had a family of his own now. A wife he adored and two sons. Twin sons.

Then, a year ago Diane had decided she wanted a little girl. Paul would've preferred to wait, space out their family, get the boys in school first. But Diane had been adamant. She'd wanted another baby. They'd argued about it, but in the end she'd convinced him. Actually, he used to joke, it was a sheer black nightie that had convinced him. The truth was, he'd never been able to refuse his wife. She was his whole world — and now she was gone.

Paul looked down at her and his heart felt the heaviness of grief. The emptiness. What would he do without Diane? How could he possibly face life without her?

Diane was at peace, but Paul was in turmoil.

The anguish rose in his throat until it escaped in a low moan. Gripping the railing of the hospital bed, he closed his eyes and felt his body rock with grief.

A sound outside the room caught his attention and he turned, recognizing Leah's voice. Leah, Diane's sister.

The two women had always been close, and it didn't surprise him that she was here. Moving from his wife's side, he opened the door to find a stricken Leah pleading with Dr. Charman.

"Paul?" She shifted her imploring gaze to him. "I woke up. Something told me to come to the hospital . . . right then . . . not to wait. I'd only been home a few hours."

Paul nodded. He hadn't been asleep long himself.

"I can't believe this," she sobbed. "Not Diane . . ." She covered her mouth, and her shoulders shook with the pain of a loss that went soul deep.

Paul opened his arms to her, and Leah walked into his embrace, but he didn't know who was comforting whom.

He needed her and she needed him.

ONE

Kelsey's weak cry stirred Paul from his light sleep. He blinked and rubbed a hand down his weary face. The midnight feedings were the worst, especially on Friday nights.

Life had fallen into a dismal pattern in the six months since Diane's funeral. He'd never worked harder in his life. Keeping up with the kids and the house and his job left room for little else. The demands seemed endless.

His family had pitched in to help every way they could. Between his mother and his sister-in-law he was managing, especially with his mother taking the kids every weekday, shuttling the boys to preschool and picking them up.

Kelsey cried again, and Paul threw aside his covers and sat on the edge of the bed. Blindly, he searched with his feet for his slippers, then stood and pulled on his robe.

Kelsey's crib was in his room, and he

automatically reached for her, placing her against his shoulder.

"Just a minute, sweetheart," he said, walking around the room until he'd located a freshly laundered diaper on top of the dresser.

Bless Leah. He didn't know what he'd do if she hadn't taken over the laundry. With so many extra medical expenses, plus the cost of the funeral, he couldn't afford a diaper service or even disposables, or, at least, not as many as he needed. At night he used the old-fashioned kind, often going through two or three. So every afternoon on her way home from teaching at the college, Leah came by to prepare dinner and start the laundry. He wouldn't have survived the past few months without Leah and his mother.

He deftly changed Kelsey's wet diaper while her bottle was heating in the microwave. He was getting fairly good at this diapering business. Early in his married life, Paul had teased Diane that she could have as many children as she wanted as long as she was the one who dealt with the messy diapers. Now changing diapers, like so many other tasks, had become his alone.

Settling in the rocking chair with Kelsey, Paul carefully touched the nipple to her lips.

The baby's tiny mouth parted, and she sucked hungrily.

He brushed the soft blond wisps of hair from her sweet face. How grateful he was that Kelsey had been born healthy. Diane had wanted a little girl so badly. An ultrasound early in the pregnancy had told them that she was to have her wish. Paul hadn't cared one way or the other, but Diane had been overjoyed at the prospect of a daughter.

Paul had been with her when Kelsey was born. Because there'd been so much concern about Diane's condition, they'd immediately handed Kelsey to him. Despite everything that had happened since, he remembered the surge of love and pride he'd experienced holding his newborn daughter that first time.

It wasn't Kelsey's fault that her birth had cost Diane her life. Not once had Paul thought to blame her. Who was there to accuse? God? Fate? Life?

Paul didn't know. He'd given up looking for answers. There wasn't enough time or energy left in a day. Not when he had to deal with the reality of raising three motherless children, aged four and less than a year.

Once Kelsey had finished the bottle, Paul held her over his shoulder again and rubbed her back. Gently rocking back and forth, he closed his eyes. He'd rest for a few minutes . . . he told himself.

Just a few minutes . . .

Saturday morning, when Leah let herself into the house that had once been her sister's, she found her brother-in-law asleep in the rocking chair, his arms cradling Kelsey.

She hesitated, not wanting to disturb him. He'd been so tired lately. They both had.

Too tired to grieve.

Too tired to do anything more than simply function, taking one step at a time, dragging from one day to the next. Moving forward, because they had no choice.

Even now, six months after her sister's death, Leah had trouble accepting the permanence of the situation. More often than she could count, Leah expected Diane to come into the room, bringing her warm smile and effervescent personality. How empty life felt without her. Empty for her.

For Paul.

For the children.

Then some days it was as if Diane was actually there. At the oddest times Leah could almost feel her sister standing beside her, thanking her for helping, for encouraging Paul.

And then there was the dream.

Leah had never told her brother-in-law about it. She'd never told anyone. It had come the night Diane died.

Paul and Leah had been at the hospital with her sister for three days, and there hadn't been any change in Diane's condition. Dr. Charman had insisted they both go home and get some sleep. Nothing was likely to happen for some time yet, he'd told them. Paul had been as reluctant to leave as Leah had, but in the end they'd both agreed.

Leah had gone to her apartment, showered and fallen into bed. She'd slept deeply, and in her dream Diane had come to her, walking through a field of wildflowers. She was barefoot and happy. Then she'd stood under a flowering magnolia tree and looked at Leah. A brilliant white light had settled above her. Diane had smiled into the light, and although Leah couldn't hear what her sister was saying, it had seemed to her that Diane was requesting a few more minutes. She'd then turned from the radiant light and smiled at Leah.

Holding a daisy, plucking at the petals, she'd told Leah how sorry she was to leave her, to leave Paul and the children. Leah had tried to interrupt, but Diane had stopped her. Her sister had explained how hard she'd battled to live, then said she'd come to understand that there was a greater wisdom in accepting death.

The problem, she whispered, was that she couldn't freely give up her life with Paul and Leah holding on to her the way they were. Holding her back. The strength of their love and their will kept her with them, prevented her from dying. It was the reason they'd been sent home. Once they were gone, she would be free.

Leah had tried to argue with her, but Diane had smiled serenely and shaken her head, claiming there wasn't enough time. She'd spoken quickly, pointing out to Leah that Paul and the children would need her help. Looking directly into Leah's eyes, she'd smiled again and asked if Leah would be willing to take her place. Leah hadn't understood then and wasn't sure she did now, but in the end she'd promised to do whatever was needed.

The next instant Leah had awakened. For a confused moment she'd lain there in bed, certain it had all been a dream. Only a dream. Yes, Diane *was* at the hospital and it *was* true that her condition was serious, but her sister *wasn't* going to die. No one had even mentioned the possibility. Quickly

Leah had gotten out of bed and rushed back to the hospital to discover that Paul was already there with Dr. Charman.

Her sister was gone.

The dream had haunted Leah for months. She'd kept her promise to Diane and was doing everything she could to help Paul with the children, but it seemed so little.

To his credit, Paul was holding up well. He was such a good father. But Leah wondered how much longer he'd be able to continue under the strain. All along, he'd been the strong one, reassuring her, reassuring his children, his parents and everyone else.

Leah didn't know how he did it. But she was grateful. His confidence was the glue that held everything together. It kept them all going — Leah, his family, everyone who was trying to help. Paul's mother took the children during the day. The cost of day care for three preschoolers was outrageous. When Paul told Leah the quotes he'd gotten from several child-care facilities, she'd thought he was joking. He couldn't survive financially paying those fees.

Because Paul's hours at the newspaper often stretched past six o'clock, Leah had gotten into the habit of picking up Kelsey and the boys at his mother's place on her way home from the college, where she taught math. Since the kids were invariably hungry, she'd start dinner. She'd also run a load or two of laundry and do whatever else she could to lighten Paul's obligations.

For six months they'd all worked together, more or less coping with everything that needed to be done. Leah, however, was growing concerned. Elizabeth Manning was a wonderful woman, but she hadn't been responsible for small children in many years, and the demands of caring for three of them were beginning to take their toll. Not only that, the older Mannings had been planning a trip to Montana to visit Paul's two sisters. Christy was pregnant with her first child, and Elizabeth Manning was hoping to be with her youngest daughter for the birth of her child.

Paul was as concerned about the situation as Leah was. Even more so. But she didn't know what he intended to do. The problem was, he probably didn't, either.

What *could* he do?

"Mommy!" Four-year-old Ryan, the older — by ten minutes — of the identical twins, came out from their bedroom, sleepily rubbing his eyes. He dragged his security blanket on the carpet behind him.

"Good morning, sweetheart," Leah said, lifting his warm little body into her arms.

"I want my mommy." Ryan's arms clasped her neck tightly.

"I know." Her voice caught as she spoke.

"When's she coming home?"

"Your mommy's in heaven now, remember?"

"But when will she come back?"

Unexpected tears filled Leah's eyes. "She won't. . . . Don't you remember what your daddy said?"

"But I *want* her to."

"I do, too." It was difficult to make Ryan and Ronnie understand, difficult to understand herself. And it didn't seem to be getting any easier.

Diane had had a husband, children, responsibilities. Her sister had been full of life and laughter. Her death made no sense to Leah. None.

Diane was blond, pretty, animated, energetic. Leah was tall and ungainly, and she lacked Diane's confidence and vivacity. At five-eight she was a full five inches taller than her younger sister had been. Her hair was a pale brown, and unlike Diane's beautiful blue eyes, hers were an indeterminate color, somewhere between green and brown depending on what she wore. Diane had been the striking one in the family.

Diane had also been the only family Leah had. Their parents had divorced when they were young, and their mother had died several years ago. They'd lost contact with their father in their teens. Any aunts, uncles, cousins, had long since faded from view.

"Are you hungry?" Leah asked Ryan, turning the conversation away from the painful subject of Diane.

Ryan's head was buried in her shoulder. He sniffled and nodded. "Can you make Egg McManning the way Mommy did?"

"Ah . . ." Leah hesitated. She had no idea what Egg McManning was. "Sure, but you'll have to show me how."

"Okay." Ryan brightened a little. "First you cook eggs and cheese and muffins, then you put everything together and eat it."

"Oh . . ." Leah was going to need a few more instructions than that. Diane had had an active imagination. She could make the most mundane chores fun and the simplest meal a feast.

"I'm hungry." Ronnie wandered out of his bedroom and into the kitchen. With both hands, he pulled out the kitchen chair, then climbed up onto the seat. He stuck his thumb in his mouth.

"Aunt Leah's making Egg McManning,"

Ryan told him.

"Good." The thumb left his mouth long enough to say that one word.

Until Diane's death Ronnie had given up sucking his thumb, but he'd started again. Leah hadn't suggested he stop and wouldn't for a while. Life had already landed him a harsh blow; she wasn't about to chastise him because he needed a little extra comfort.

"Did I hear someone mention Egg Mc-Manning for breakfast?" Paul stood in the kitchen doorway, Kelsey on his shoulder, sleeping soundly.

"Aunt Leah's making them for us," Ryan explained solemnly.

"I hope you'll share the recipe with me," she muttered under her breath.

"Toast English muffins," Paul said between yawns, "add some scrambled egg, a slice of cheese and voilà." He pressed his free hand to his mouth, stifling another yawn. "How long have you been here?"

"Only a few minutes." Leah had her back to him, searching the contents of the refrigerator for a carton of eggs.

"I thought you couldn't come until noon today."

"I lied," she said over her shoulder, giving him a quick grin. "I cleaned up my place last night and figured I'd get a head start with the kids this morning." She set the eggs, muffins and cheese on the counter. "I thought Ryan and Ronnie might enjoy a trip to the zoo." Out of the corner of her eye she watched for the twins' reaction.

"The zoo?" Ronnie asked excitedly. "With lions and tigers and bears?"

"Didn't you have a date last night?" Paul asked, frowning.

"I was too tired to go out." She grabbed a skillet that had been left to dry in the rack next to the sink and set it on the stove.

"If you were so tired, where'd you find the energy to clean house?"

Paul was like that sometimes. Leah guessed it was the reporter in him. He'd prod until he got the answer he already knew to be the truth.

"If I were you," she said, waving a spatula at him, "I wouldn't look a gift horse in the mouth."

"I know what you're doing." Fierce pride brightened his blue eyes.

"So do I," she countered smoothly. "I'm cooking breakfast for two hungry little boys."

Kelsey woke and started whimpering. Leah got the impression that Paul would've preferred to continue their conversation, but didn't know which to do first, deal with his daughter or talk to Leah. "But —"

"I'll heat her bottle for you," she offered, cutting off his reply.

Paul looked haggard. She'd purposely come to the house early so he could have part of the day to himself. The guy was exhausted. They all were. But for Leah there was an escape. At the end of the day she went home to her apartment, free from the demands of three small, needy children. A place of her own where she could find peace and privacy. Paul had no such deliverance.

Breakfast was ready when he returned with a freshly diapered Kelsey. He'd taken the time to dress in jeans and a sweatshirt, Leah saw, glancing in his direction.

She set three plates on the table and reached for Kelsey, tucking the baby in her arms and smiling as she eagerly began to gulp down her formula.

"You're ruining your social life," Paul said, biting into the muffin as though it had been days since his last meal.

"No, I'm not." There wasn't any social life to ruin, Leah thought. She only dated occasionally. Rob was a friend and would never be anything more. They had a good time together, but canceling an evening with him wasn't a big deal.

"You should've gone out last night," Paul

said stubbornly.

"I wasn't in the mood." She stroked the side of Kelsey's face, her heart constricting as she noticed her resemblance to Diane. The little chin, the shape of her ears . . .

"Leah, please don't." The earnestness in Paul's voice caught her attention. Slowly she lifted her eyes to his.

"I feel guilty enough knowing what this is doing to my parents," he said. "Please, don't you sacrifice yourself for me, too."

"It's not for you," she told him. "It's for Ryan, Ronnie and Kelsey. And it isn't a sacrifice. If the situation were reversed, Diane wouldn't think twice about doing the same for me. She'd *expect* me to help."

Paul closed his eyes and nodded, his face grim. "I still don't feel good about it."

"I know." Leah did; she knew it went against Paul's pride to rely on his family so much. He didn't have any choice, but he didn't like it.

Not one bit.

Paul was in an angry, unreasonable mood. If there was anything to be grateful for, it was that Leah had taken the boys to the zoo and Kelsey was napping.

He would've liked nothing better than to sit down at his computer. He was five chapters into a book, but he hadn't written a word since Diane's death. How could he? There hadn't been a moment he could call his own. Not that he'd been in the state of mind that would allow him to get absorbed in his novel anyway. But he wanted to try, as much for Diane, who'd loved this story, as himself.

His two younger brothers had asked him to join their softball team. He felt a bit guilty for spurning Jason and Rich's efforts to divert him, but feeling like a charity case was worse.

In any event, there wouldn't have been time for softball this Saturday, since a dozen chores around the house needed to be done.

One of the twins had pulled the towel rack off the bathroom wall. When he'd asked who was responsible, both Ryan and Ronnie had claimed, "not me." *Not me* seemed to have a lot to answer for lately.

Once he'd finished the bathroom repair, Paul moved into the twins' bedroom, where the closet door was off the track. Setting it back in place wasn't a simple task. Again and again he struggled to fit it onto the narrow groove until it was all he could do not to rip the door out in his frustration.

"You're losing it, old boy," he said, forcing himself to step back and take several deep breaths. Calmer now, he finally succeeded in fixing it.

From there, Paul moved to the garage. His car needed an oil change, and although he'd gotten in the habit of going to a twenty-minute lube place, this time he decided to do it himself, hoping to save a few dollars.

Tinkering in the garage, he realized he needed a few things from the hardware store. No big deal. He'd be back in fifteen, twenty minutes tops. It wasn't until he'd gone a block down the road that he remembered Kelsey.

He tore back to the house like a madman and raced inside the front door, his heart pounding so hard it sounded like thunder in his ear.

Kelsey was sleeping soundly, completely unaware that her own father had actually forgotten her.

Slumping into the rocking chair, Paul clenched his fists, resisting the urge to plow one through the wall. Paul had never been a violent man, and he was horrified by the rage that surged through him.

Leah's timing couldn't have been worse. The boys exploded through the front door, happy and excited. Ryan and Ronnie were each clutching a bright red balloon in one hand and an ice-cream cone in the other.

"Daddy! Daddy, guess what we saw?"

Paul didn't answer, but that didn't seem to dampen Ryan's enthusiasm.

"There was an eagle, a great big one with wings as long as . . . as an airplane and claws like this." He formed his small hand into the shape. "Bigger even."

"Paul, what's wrong?" Leah's soft voice came to him. If he closed his eyes, he could almost believe it was Diane speaking to him — only it wasn't.

"I left the house to do one small errand," he said in a low voice.

"Yes?"

"I went without Kelsey. I left her in the house alone," he said. "Anything could've happened, don't you understand? I left my own daughter behind . . . I completely forgot about her."

"Nothing happened. It's not the end of the world."

"Isn't it?" he shouted.

Leah steered the boys toward the kitchen. "Finish your ice cream at the table, then wash your hands," she told them calmly. "After that, it's time for your nap."

"Ronnie, get your thumb out of your mouth," Paul yelled. "You're too old to be sucking your thumb."

The boy raised stricken eyes to his father

29

and rushed into the other room.

"Take a few minutes to relax," Leah told Paul, "and I'll bring you a cup of tea."

"I don't want any tea."

"I know," she said. "You want Diane back. We all do."

"A cup of tea isn't going to help."

"Perhaps not, but we need to talk, and anytime Diane had something important she wanted to discuss, she did it over a cup of tea."

Paul didn't need his sister-in-law to tell him about his dead wife's habits. For an instant he wanted to lash out at her, the same way he had at Ronnie. But the guilt he felt at his irrational anger compounded as he followed Leah into the kitchen. Ryan and Ronnie were sitting at the table. Their excitement was gone, their shoulders hunched forward. Paul leaned over and kissed Ronnie's cheek. "I'm sorry I snapped at you."

"I won't suck my thumb anymore," the four-year-old promised tearfully.

Ryan scooted off the chair and raced to their bedroom, returning with his yellow blanket, which he indignantly handed Paul. "If Ronnie can't have his thumb, then I don't want my blankie."

"You're sure?" Paul asked. Ryan hadn't

slept without his blanket since Diane's death.

"Yes."

"If you're finished, go wash your hands," Leah told the boys. "Naptime."

Paul expected an argument. The boys rarely went to sleep without a fuss these days. They seemed to feel that if they were old enough for kindergarten in September, they were old enough to forgo afternoon naps. To his surprise neither one voiced a protest.

He was left alone in the kitchen as Leah walked the boys down the hallway. She returned a couple of minutes later and poured them each a cup of hot tea.

She was about to sit down when Ryan stalked back into the kitchen, glaring at his father. Here it comes, Paul thought. The argument about naptime.

"What is it?" Paul demanded impatiently.

Ryan blinked, pointing at the blanket on the chair next to Paul. "Ronnie's got his thumb in his mouth so I want my blankie back." He grabbed the tattered yellow blanket and raced to his bedroom again.

Leah was smiling, and if he'd been in a better mood, Paul would've found humor in it, too.

"So you had a good time at the zoo?" he

managed to ask politely.

"Yes. The boys were great." She stared down at the delicate teacup in her hands. "Listen, Paul, I've been doing some thinking about the situation here, with you and the kids, and it seems to me we need to come up with some solutions."

"*We?* This isn't your problem."

"Yes, it is, although I hesitate to call it a problem."

"Then what would you call it?"

"An opportunity."

"An opportunity for what?" he asked, hating the way he'd raised his voice. The anger he felt simmered just below the surface, and seemed ready to burst forth at the slightest provocation.

"I've given a lot of thought to what I'm about to propose."

"Leah, listen, forgive me, I'm in a foul mood. Not good company. I don't know what's wrong with me, but —"

"I know what's wrong. What's wrong with all of us. Why Ronnie's started sucking his thumb again and why Ryan can't get to sleep unless he's got his blankie."

"It's Diane. . . ."

She nodded. "We all miss her, we all need her, but she isn't here and we have to adjust. It's going to take time and patience."

"I've run out of both," Paul admitted wryly.

"So have I," she acknowledged, surprising him. "That's why I want to give my notice at the college and move in with you and the kids."

Two

"I won't hear of it," Paul said bluntly, emphatically.

Leah had expected an argument. Paul was proud. Being forced to accept her help, or anyone's for that matter, conflicted with his independent nature. He'd been forced to rely on her and his parents for the past six months, which was difficult enough.

"I've considered this very seriously," Leah said.

"I appreciate the offer, but I can't allow you to do it." Paul shook his head. Others might have buckled under at the obstinate look in his deep blue eyes, but Leah had come to know her brother-in-law too well to surrender that easily.

"The boys aren't adjusting."

"Leah, I said no," he returned firmly.

"Ryan can barely leave the house without his blanket. We both know he has trouble going to sleep without it."

"In time he'll give it up."

"And Ronnie's taken to sucking his thumb again," she continued undaunted. "In case you haven't noticed, he's become ambidextrous, although he continues to favor his right hand."

"Both thumbs?" Paul didn't bother to disguise his shock. His eyes hardened as he said, "In time the boys will learn to adjust."

"They need stability and security."

"I'm trying," Paul said, inhaling sharply. "I'm doing everything I can."

"No one's blaming you."

"I can't do everything."

"And that's my point," Leah told him quietly. "No one expects you to. My moving in will only be temporary. It'll give the boys a chance to adjust to Diane's loss without all the upheaval they're going through now. It'll help regulate Kelsey's schedule, too."

"What's wrong with her schedule?" Paul demanded.

Leah didn't want to sound critical of his efforts, but, in fact, Kelsey didn't *have* much of a schedule.

"It's . . . erratic. Especially at night."

"But she wakes up and —"

"You *expect* her to wake up and you're so attuned to the slightest noise that when she does, you spring out of bed instantly."

"I had to put her crib in my room," he said, "otherwise I didn't hear her."

"I'm just explaining that you need to move her into her own room and start regulating her eating schedule a little more." She paused. "I can help you do that."

He sighed wearily but didn't respond.

"It'd only be for a few years," Leah murmured.

"You don't really think I'm going to agree to this, do you?"

"Just until the boys are in school full-time and Kelsey's in preschool. By then the kids won't need me as much and I'll be able to resume my teaching career."

Paul didn't say anything for several minutes, weighing her words. "No," he finally said. "I appreciate this more than you'll ever realize, but I can't let you do it. It's too much of a sacrifice."

"Diane was my sister," Leah said softly, hoping to hide the pain that surfaced whenever she mentioned her sister's name. "Her children are the only family I have left. It wouldn't be a sacrifice — it would be something done willingly and out of love. The twins need me and so does Kelsey."

"But it's not fair for you to give up your life."

"Give it up?" she repeated with a short

laugh. "You make it sound like I'm offering to leap into a volcano to appease some ancient god. I'm going to take a leave of absence from teaching. That's all."

"You won't be spending your time traveling or studying, though, will you?"

"No, but I'll gain more from the experience than you think. I love the children. I really want to do this."

"What about money?"

It went without saying that finances were currently tight for Paul. He couldn't pay Leah, nor could he offer to reimburse her for lost wages, but she'd taken all of that into account.

"I'll be giving up my apartment, so I'll be saving on rent. Plus, I have a small trust fund from my mother and grandmother. It isn't a lot, but it's enough for the next couple of years."

Paul hesitated, his jaw tensing before he slowly shook his head. "Your offer touches me deeply, but I just can't let you do it."

Leah knew it would eventually come down to this. She knew she'd have to bring up the subject of Eric and Elizabeth Manning.

"What about your parents?" Although Leah preferred not to drag them into the discussion, she had no choice. Paul's parents had retired several years before and enjoyed traveling in their motor home. But since Diane's death they'd stayed in Seattle to help Paul with the children. She'd been unable to visit Taylor, her oldest daughter, when little Eric was born. Now Christy was pregnant and it looked as if, once again, Elizabeth wouldn't be there for the birth of a grandchild.

"I've been checking into having someone from church watch the kids while Mom and Dad are away," Paul informed her stiffly.

"Strangers?" Leah raised her eyebrows.

"What else can I do?" he flared.

"Let me move in with you. It's the obvious answer. The kids love me and I love them. They'll be in their own home, with their own toys. They've had enough disruption in their lives already. I know how hard this is for you, Paul, but you can't let your pride stand in the way of what's best for your children."

He stood abruptly and walked to the far side of the kitchen. "It seems so unfair to *you.*"

"But I'd consider it a privilege. I don't expect there'll be many other opportunities in my life to do something like this for those I love. My being here with the kids can make a difference. It can help them adjust to the loss of their mother. Please believe

38

me, it isn't a sacrifice, it's an honor. Years from now I'll be able to look back and feel good about the contribution I made to shaping my sister's children, to helping them through this difficult time."

Paul rubbed his face with both hands. "I don't know."

He was weakening — Leah could see it, although he was still struggling with his pride, his natural inclination to carry everything on his own shoulders.

"It won't be for more than a few years," she reiterated.

"What about you and Rob?"

Leah smiled to herself. She'd been dating Rob Mullins for three years. They were both members of the math department at Highline Community College and shared a number of interests. Above all, they were friends. If they were going to marry, they would have done so long before now. "What about him?" she asked.

"What does he think of this?"

"I didn't ask him."

Paul's eyes widened.

"Rob'll understand," she assured him. Leah didn't feel it was necessary to go into the intricacies of their relationship. They dated more for the sake of companionship and convenience than romance. Rob was divorced and had been for fifteen years. If he wanted to remarry, he would've brought up the subject long ago.

"How can you be so sure he won't mind? If I was dating Diane right now, I can tell you I wouldn't take kindly to her moving in with her brother-in-law — no matter what the circumstances."

"You're not Rob. And I'm not Diane. . . ."

"He'll care."

Leah ignored his concern. "There's only a couple of weeks left in the term, and I've already talked this over with Dean Mac-Kenzie. I told him there's a strong possibility I wouldn't be returning for at least a year. But he needs to know for certain."

Paul didn't say anything for several minutes. He walked over to the teapot, carried it back to the table and refilled their cups. "I don't have a good feeling about this."

"But you'll agree to let me move in with you?"

He nodded slowly. "And I'll thank God every day for a sister-in-law as unselfish as you."

"What's this?" Ryan asked, lifting a textbook from one of the boxes neatly stacked in the corner of Leah's closet.

Each of the four bedrooms was now in

use. Leah took the one across from the nursery and next to the twins' room. The master bedroom, where Paul slept, was at the far end of the long hallway.

"A book," she said as she unpacked her suitcase. She hung up one item at a time as the boys investigated several of the heavy cartons she'd brought with her. Most of her furniture had gone into storage, but she hadn't been able to part with some of her precious books. She probably wouldn't have the time or the energy to explore propositional calculus in the next couple of years; nevertheless, she'd hauled several boxes of books from her office.

"I like books," Ronnie said, taking his thumb out of his mouth long enough to tell her. He sat on the carpet next to his brother, tucking his legs beneath him. Ryan held his tattered yellow blanket under his arm as he leafed through the text, carefully examining each page as though he understood the concepts. Leah didn't have the heart to tell him he was holding it upside down.

"After dinner I'll read you a story," she promised them.

"Mommy used to read to us."

The memory of Diane sitting with her sons flashed into Leah's mind. She remembered her sister sitting on the living-room couch with the twins on either side. A large book of nursery rhymes was spread open across her lap as she read aloud. The boys nestled against her, half-asleep.

The injustice of her sister's death, the heartlessness of it, struck an unexpected blow. Leah paused in her task, holding a silk blouse to her stomach until the disturbing image passed.

"Are you going to be our mommy now?" Ryan asked, looking up at her with wide blue eyes. Paul's eyes. Both boys had been blessed with the same incredibly blue eyes as their father. Leah wasn't sure she'd ever seen eyes that precise color. It was the first thing she noticed whenever she met any of the Manning family.

"Mommy's in heaven," Ronnie said, poking his brother with his elbow.

Ryan went still for a moment and shut his eyes tightly. "Sometimes I forget what she looks like. I have to try real hard to remember."

"Here," Leah said, sitting on the end of the bed, eager to prompt the boys' memory. She reached for her purse and withdrew her wallet. Inside were several pictures of Diane, Paul and the twins. She took them out of the plastic case and handed them to the boys, who'd gathered beside her.

"How come she's so fat?" Ryan asked, pointing to the first picture.

Leah smiled. "That's because you and your brother were growing inside her tummy," she explained, ruffling Ryan's blond hair.

"I don't 'member that."

"I don't suppose you do."

"Kelsey was inside her tummy, too."

"Yes, she was," Leah said, picking up Ronnie and settling him on her lap. "Here's a picture of the two of you when you were born." They were dressed in white T-shirts with protective cuffs over their tiny hands. A small blue ribbon was taped in each baby's fuzzy blond hair.

"Which one's me?" Ryan asked.

"That one." Leah pointed to the infant on the left, although she didn't actually know.

"What's this picture?" Ronnie asked, pulling the bottom one free from Leah's hand. She had to look herself before she could say.

"That, my young man, was taken at Easter a few years ago." She grinned, remembering how the candy-filled baskets she'd brought the boys had been bigger than they were. Ryan and Ronnie were toddling toward her when she'd snapped the picture. It was one of Leah's favorites.

She shuffled through the other photographs, and paused as she came upon one of Paul and Diane together. Paul's eyes held Diane's, and it was clear how much in love they were. Leah's heart constricted. It seemed so unfair that Paul should lose Diane. Six months after her death he was still grieving as though it had happened only yesterday. But then, so was she.

Leah often had questions about Diane's death. Not medical questions, but . . . spiritual ones. She didn't know what other word to use. She'd never told Paul, never told anyone, about the dream.

In some ways it was what prompted her to suggest she move in with Paul and the children. It was during the dream that Diane had asked Leah to take her place.

In retrospect Leah wished she'd questioned Diane, argued with her, convinced her to stay. Even after all these months, that vision of Diane haunted Leah. Sometimes she believed it was a product of her own imagination. Other times, she was sure it was real.

At any rate, Leah had kept her word. She'd moved in with Diane's family and was taking her sister's place — as a mother, but certainly not as a wife. Even with the kids, she felt woefully inadequate.

Leah didn't know how she, a single woman, a college-level math professor, was supposed to deal with three small children on a daily basis. She didn't have all the answers, only the determination to keep her promise to Diane.

There was bound to be a period of adjustment for them all, Leah realized. Paul was grateful for her help, but at the same time resentful that he needed her. And he *did* need her, no question there. Still, it would take a while for him to get over that.

Leah respected Paul. He'd loved her sister, still loved her, and was a good father. Although she didn't have much in common with him, other than their love for the children, for now that was enough.

"Tell you what we'll do," Leah said, tucking her arms around the children and bringing them close to her side. "We'll find some pictures of your mommy and put them up in your room, so you won't forget what she looks like. How does that sound?"

"Can we put up a picture of me, too?" Ryan asked. "So Mommy won't forget what *we* look like?"

"Yes, sweetheart, we can," she whispered, kissing the top of his head.

"Where is everyone?" Paul's voice came from the kitchen.

Leah glanced at her watch. She'd been so busy unpacking, the time had slipped away from her. Before she could get off the bed, Paul was standing in the bedroom doorway.

He wore his trench coat, a gift from Diane when he'd been hired by the Seattle daily paper. What decent journalist didn't own a trench coat, she'd teased.

"Ah-ha, here you are," Paul said, crouching down and holding out his arms to his sons. Ryan and Ronnie ran across the room to hurl themselves into their father's embrace. With a growl Paul stood, lifting both boys off the floor and hugging them close.

"Where's Kelsey?" he asked, lowering the boys.

"Napping." Although now that Leah noted the time, she realized Kelsey was probably awake. She moved into the nursery, and sure enough, the little girl was lying on her back, her hands fluttering gaily. Leah picked her up.

"I see you got everything moved in all right," Paul said, following her into the nursery.

"Almost everything. I'll need to make one last trip in the morning, but that should do it."

"You've got enough room for everything?"

"Plenty," she assured him. Enough room

in her heart to nurture these precious children. And what else really mattered?

"Dinner's just about ready," Leah said as she set Kelsey on the changing table and began to remove her soggy diaper.

"I can do it," Paul said, taking over. "You must be exhausted."

"I'm fine, really." But she didn't protest. Giving him some time alone with his daughter, Leah walked into the kitchen.

It was even more difficult for Paul to accept her help now that she was living in his home. She hoped he'd grow accustomed to her being there and wouldn't feel the need to repay her for the "sacrifice" she'd made. Although she'd tried repeatedly, she couldn't make him understand that she didn't consider this an imposition. It was her idea, after all, as she'd reminded him more than once.

Dinner was on the table a few minutes later. Leah had never been much of a cook. There'd been no reason to develop that skill when the only one she was feeding was herself. Until recently, she'd survived on frozen entrées and fast-food dinners. Diane used to claim her unhealthy eating habits would be the end of her. But it wasn't Leah who'd left behind an anguished family.

When they were finished with dinner — a

basic chili and an uninspired salad — Paul cleared the table while Leah stacked the dishes in the dishwasher. Wordlessly they worked together while Ryan and Ronnie entertained their sister.

"I wish you'd let me do that," he said as she scrubbed a pot.

"I don't mind." There were only a handful of dishes that needed to be washed by hand, and she'd be done in a few minutes.

"Perhaps *you* don't mind, but *I* do," Paul said, his words taut.

The stark tone of his voice surprised Leah. It wasn't going to be easy, the two of them adjusting to each other's presence.

"All right," she agreed amicably enough. She didn't know what Paul thought of her. She wondered if he had any feelings toward her, one way or the other.

They'd worked together, talked occasionally, grieved together, wept in each other's arms — but when it came to defining their relationship, Leah was at a loss.

She turned off the water and dried her hands. Replacing the dish towel on the wire rack, she glanced over at Paul, her eyes skimming his. In that one brief glance, she saw so much. His fatigue. His pain. His regret.

She was about to leave the room when

Paul caught her by the arm. He dropped his hand almost immediately, and for a moment he said nothing. But his meaning was clear.

He was sorry for speaking harshly to her. Leah knew that as surely as she'd ever known anything. Something deep inside her longed to comfort him, assure him that she understood.

The days might pass. But the pain didn't.

"I didn't mean to snap at you," he said.

"I know."

"It's just that . . ."

"I *know,* Paul. You don't have to explain. You're grateful I'm here and at the same time you wish I wasn't. You aren't going to hurt my feelings. I understand."

Leah did understand; nevertheless his words a few minutes ago had hurt. She knew Paul hadn't meant to be insensitive, and he wasn't unfeeling. But his response to her being there, performing the tasks that had once been his wife's, left her feeling unwanted. Diane was the one he wanted, not Leah.

His reaction stirred once-forgotten inadequacies and brought to life deeply buried resentments, not toward Diane, but toward their mother. Diane had been the beautiful child; Leah was plain, inept. While Diane

49

had been a high school cheerleader, Leah had been shy, studious, a plain Jane. Leah knew she'd embarrassed her mother. Diane was her golden girl, Leah ordinary and unattractive.

The way their mother had favored one sister over the other had hurt Diane more than it had Leah. Leah had worked hard at her studies, received a full scholarship to the University of Washington and graduated with honors. By then their mother was gone, but Diane had been there to cheer her success. She'd always been there to boost Leah's self-confidence.

But she wasn't there anymore.

Later that night, after the boys and Kelsey were asleep, Paul brought Leah a cup of coffee. She was sitting in front of the television mindlessly watching some sitcom, too tired to move. She was physically and mentally exhausted.

For months Paul had carried all responsibility for these children. Leah didn't know how he'd managed for so long.

"Thanks," she said, accepting the steaming mug.

"You look beat."

"I was just wondering where the boys get their energy."

"They're a handful, aren't they?" His smile was filled with fatherly pride, and Leah found herself responding with a smile of her own.

Paul settled on the recliner across from her. He was a good-looking man. His features were imperfect, rugged, but nevertheless appealing. Or maybe appealing *because* of that. It was easy to understand why Diane had fallen in love with him.

Leah would never forget the day Diane had called her from Alaska nearly seven years ago. She'd phoned to tell her she'd married Paul Manning. Leah had been aghast. She'd never met Paul, and her sister, after an all-too-brief courtship, had decided to marry him. Leah was, to say the least, shaken.

They'd always been close. It had hurt that her sister would marry this man without even talking it over. For a time Leah had been furious. Meeting Paul had only partially appeased her. Eventually, though, she'd seen that despite Diane's age, it was a solid marriage. The fact that Paul so obviously loved her had gone a long way toward reassuring Leah.

"You'll get used to the boys' antics," Paul said, interrupting her thoughts. "Does Ryan usually take his stuffed animals in the bathtub with him?"

Paul grinned. "Not usually."

"I see. So what happened tonight was in my honor?"

"Don't worry, they'll dry. A little the worse for wear, but they will dry."

"What about his blankie? We can't wash it?" Leah hadn't been able to persuade Ryan to let go of it for even an hour to run it through the washing machine. Whenever she suggested it, the four-year-old clung to his stained, torn blanket as if she'd proposed burning the thing — which might not be such a bad idea.

Paul rolled his eyes. "At least Ronnie's thumbs are clean."

Leah chuckled, but she worried about the boys and their unabated need for reassurance.

"We're going to be all right," Paul said, closing his eyes and leaning his head against the back of his chair. "There were days I wondered but now, for the first time since the funeral, I believe it."

"Me, too."

Paul sighed, straightened, then took a sip of his coffee. After a moment he stared blankly at the television screen.

"I miss Diane most right about now," he said, his voice low. "We used to sit and talk every night after the boys were asleep. She'd tell me about her day, and I'd talk to her about mine. I'd hold her in my arms and we'd relax together, on that sofa you're sitting on now." He shook his head. "I've tried a hundred times to remember the things we said, to resurrect the good feelings I had holding her in my arms. But you know, I can't remember a single word of our conversations."

"It was just having her there, listening, that was important."

Paul nodded. "I suppose you're right." But he didn't sound convinced.

They didn't often talk about Diane. She guessed it was natural that it would happen tonight, her first night in his home.

"You know what *I* miss about her most?" Leah asked.

"No."

"Shopping at the mall."

Paul chuckled. "I should've guessed. I've never been able to understand what it is about shopping that intrigues you women."

"Diane had an incredible knack for finding a bargain."

"You mean she had an incredible knack for spending money, don't you?"

Leah folded her legs under her and smiled. "It wasn't so much the shopping, but the time we spent laughing when we tried on clothes and ordered cheesecake for lunch and then, because we felt guilty, salad for dessert."

Leah's stomach tensed at the pain that came into Paul's eyes. A look that was reflected in her own.

It was supposed to get easier, but she'd never missed her sister more than she did at that moment. Missing Diane hurt so much. For months, Leah had kept the ache of loneliness to herself, not daring to discuss it with Paul, knowing that he, too, was overwhelmed by pain. It was oddly freeing to release some of her own anguish now. To reveal it to the one person who'd completely understand.

"We're going to be all right," Paul said again.

"Yes, I think we will," she murmured.

In their own ways they were coping. How well remained to be seen.

For a long while Paul said nothing.

Neither did Leah.

Paul finished his coffee, then set aside his mug, closing his eyes, visibly relaxed.

Leah finished her coffee too, knowing that if she didn't go to bed immediately, she'd fall asleep right there on the couch.

The day had been even more tiring than she'd realized. Her bones ached from the exertion of moving. From the fatigue of dealing with the unending demands of two preschoolers and an infant.

"Good night, Paul," she said, unfolding her legs and standing awkwardly. Her feet didn't seem to want to cooperate.

" 'Night, Diane."

THREE

Diane.

Paul's eyes shot open. For a moment it had almost seemed as if Diane was in the living room with him. As if he were chuckling over Ryan's mischievous nature with his much-loved wife. Then . . . a slip of the tongue had nearly crippled him with grief.

For an agonizing moment he was at a loss for words. It had been a natural mistake, he supposed. Under the circumstances an understandable mistake. Certainly a forgivable one.

"I'm sorry," he said, looking at Leah, hoping he hadn't offended her.

"No problem," she reassured him with a smile. She headed toward her bedroom.

Paul reached for his coffee and saw that his hand was shaking as he raised the mug to his lips.

Diane.

Sometimes he wondered if the ache of her

56

loss would ever ease. She'd been gone half a year, yet his grief was as powerful now as it had been that night, the night of her death.

In the time since her funeral, Paul had experienced the full range of emotions. Unleashed fear. Burning anger. Intense sadness. And occasionally a sort of acceptance. Just when he felt he'd moved beyond the pain, something else would happen, and he'd have to deal with each series of emotions all over again, as if facing them for the first time.

He was grateful to Leah, although he hadn't been nearly as gracious as he should've been when she'd offered to move in. He liked Diane's older sister. She was a generous woman, and he'd always be grateful to her for the commitment she'd made to him and the children. Frankly Paul didn't know what he would've done without her.

He recalled the first time he'd met Leah, and how surprised he'd been. He'd expected another Diane. Someone so full of life and laughter that her smile rivaled the brilliance of the sun. He'd imagined she'd be as blond and pretty as his young wife.

Leah was none of those things.

She wasn't unattractive; he wouldn't even describe her as plain. As a writer he should be able to find the right words, yet each one that came to him, he ended up discarding. At one time he'd thought of her as nondescript.

He'd since changed his mind.

There was a subdued radiance to her, a joy that broke through her restraint every so often when he wasn't expecting to see it. It never failed to charm him.

She'd always been Ryan and Ronnie's favorite relative. It had been Leah who'd comforted them when they learned about their mother. It had been Leah who'd encouraged them when Paul had no encouragement to give. It had been Leah who'd cheered them when he didn't know if he'd ever have the strength to laugh again.

That afternoon had been a good example. He'd returned from the office to find her in her bedroom, with the boys gathered around. When he'd walked in, she'd looked up and smiled . . . and for a moment, the briefest of moments, Paul had felt whole again.

Over coffee that evening he'd experienced that same sense of wholeness, as though the crushing weight he'd been carrying since Diane's death had been eased. Not by much, but enough for some of the numbness to leave his heart.

He owed Leah a debt he couldn't repay in

several lifetimes. Although he didn't want to admit it, he was glad she was there with him and the children. He'd promised himself he wouldn't take advantage of her generosity. He'd make sure she had time to herself, time to get away, socialize — do whatever she needed to do to keep her sanity during the next two years.

Her sanity, after all, was essential to his.

A month passed, the easiest weeks for Paul since Diane's death. Each day he felt less embittered, less confused, less depressed. He'd even started thinking about working on his novel again. The anticipation cheered him.

The transition from college professor to housekeeper–mother must've been hard for Leah, but she was managing exceptionally well. Paul was proud of her, proud of the progress she'd made. Her efforts around the house had made a tremendous difference. She'd begun some of the yard work, too, and with Ryan and Ronnie's "help" was planting a garden.

All three children were thriving under her attention and care. Paul couldn't believe the difference in his sons. Ryan actually forgot his blankie sometimes. He was watching cartoons without it one afternoon when

Paul had arrived home from work. Ronnie was beside him, and for the first time in recent memory, his son's thumb wasn't in his mouth.

Paul had praised Leah, but she'd quickly dismissed his compliments, claiming the changes in the boys' behavior weren't due solely to her. Although the boys were more secure now that she was there to take care of them, attending the preschool with their neighborhood friends had helped, too. And the summer sunshine, she said, had also contributed.

Although Paul didn't really agree with her, he'd let it pass. He definitely attributed the boys' improvement to Leah, but he knew she wasn't comfortable with his appreciation.

He used to think of her as quiet and unassuming. But in the past few weeks he'd realized she was more than that. She was sensitive and loving, and her gentleness was a balm that was healing them all.

The phone on his desk rang, and Paul reached for it.

"Hi there, big brother," a deep voice greeted him.

"Rich, hello." Paul hadn't heard from his brothers much lately. Mostly it was his fault. He'd rejected their efforts to draw him out after Diane's death. Both Rich and Jason were on a softball team and they'd wanted him to join them in a summer league. Paul had nearly laughed out loud. There wasn't time for sports in his life. And the thought of playing softball had seemed ludicrous, considering the loss he'd endured. Paul understood that Rich and Jason were only trying to help, but he hadn't been ready.

"Rich, it's good to hear from you," Paul said, meaning it.

"You might have called me," his brother responded. "I've left you enough messages."

"I know. I'm sorry."

"You're fortunate I'm willing to let you make it up to me."

"I figured you would."

"I'm calling to ask sort of a favor." Some of the teasing left Rich's voice.

"Oh?"

"One of the guys on the softball team, John Duncan — you remember John, don't you? The mechanic from the garage off Seventy-sixth?"

"Yeah." Paul vaguely recalled meeting the guy. "What about him?"

"He has to miss the next two or three games. Jason and I were talking it over and we thought . . . since Leah's taking care of the kids now, maybe you could get away for a couple of Saturday mornings. If you have to bring the twins, that'd be okay, too. Jamie always comes to the games and I'm sure she wouldn't mind looking after them."

Despite himself, Paul chuckled.

"What's so funny?"

"Richard, Richard, haven't you learned yet?"

"Learned what?"

"Not to volunteer your wife for something until you've checked with her first."

"Oh . . . right. Listen, the team's desperate. John's a good shortstop, but not as good as you."

"Do you suppose buttering me up's going to help?"

"I was hoping it would," Rich admitted honestly. "Can you do it?"

"Let me get back to you."

"When?"

"This evening," Paul promised.

He was tempted. Leah would encourage him to do it; he knew that without asking.

Maybe he would, Paul decided. Maybe he would.

"You're positive you don't mind?" Paul asked for the third time the following Saturday morning. He couldn't help feeling guilty about abandoning Leah with the kids while he went off to play softball.

"Paul," she chided, smiling up at him. "Go, before I push you out the door. Don't worry about us. The boys and I will have lots of fun."

"Planting a garden sounds more like work to me." A half dozen egg cartons cluttered the kitchen counter. Leah and the boys had been enthusiastically working on this project for weeks.

Somehow they'd gotten him involved. Two weekends before, he'd found himself spading up a section of the yard for them to use. When he'd finished, Leah and the boys had dumped topsoil and fertilizer on the rough earth, spreading it out as evenly as they could.

Then the eggshells started turning up. One afternoon the three of them had been engrossed in filling halves of eggshells with potting soil and then inserting a single seed. Now the tiny zucchini, cucumber, radish and lettuce sprouts poked out of the shells.

The seedlings, Leah declared that morning, were now strong enough to be planted outside.

Paul's sons had been delighted with the idea. More than once he'd seen the two of them peering over the kitchen counter, as if they were hoping to catch the seeds bursting instantly into full-grown plants.

"I could bring Kelsey with me," he offered.

"Then she'll go down late for her nap and be crabby. You don't need that." She carried the boys' empty cereal bowls to the sink. "Now, hurry or you'll be late."

Paul drank the last of his coffee. As she strolled past, Leah grabbed the bill of his baseball cap and pushed it down, past his eyes. "Have fun, Mickey Mantle," she teased.

Paul laughed, straightened the cap and grabbed his mitt. It wasn't until he was outside starting his car that he realized he hadn't felt so lighthearted in a long time.

Paul's softball skills were a bit rusty, but he made a diving catch and caught a ground ball that turned the tide of the game. His brothers and temporary teammates slapped him on the back and ran off the field with him.

It felt great to get out like this. To laugh. Strangely, perhaps, he didn't feel guilty about having fun. It felt right to be with his brothers.

Jamie, Rich's wife, had packed a picnic lunch for after the game. She invited Paul to join her, Jason and Rich, but he declined, anxious to return home. Jamie and Rich's little girl, Bethany, was spending the day with Jamie's mother, so they were free to enjoy an all-adults afternoon.

Jason had eagerly accepted their invitation, and Paul was glad to see it — his two brothers together — his sister-in-law so pleasant and kind. Although Jamie had been part of the family for almost two years, it never ceased to surprise him that his play-the-field brother had married her. Of the three of them, Rich had been blessed with the best looks. His tall, compelling presence had garnered him attention from the opposite sex since high school. In fact, that was where he and Jamie had become friends. Good friends. And their friendship had eventually led to marriage.

Paul liked his sister-in-law a great deal. Compared to Rich's other girlfriends, she seemed so . . . unpretentious, even a little ordinary. In many ways she was like Leah.

He sighed as he thought of Diane's sister. Leah, ordinary? There was nothing ordinary about her! And, to be fair, Jamie was pretty special, too. Maybe it was that still-waters-run-deep thing, but these were self-confident, compassionate women, both of them.

A grateful tenderness took hold of him as he considered the changes Leah had brought to his life in the past month. The changes she'd made in his children's lives. Her warmth had largely gone unnoticed by him until she'd moved in. Her optimism. Her smile, too.

There was something about her smile that defied description. The way it subtly lifted the corners of her mouth and then made its way into her eyes. He'd always thought Leah's eyes were plain, an unremarkable hazel. Now he knew better, and he found her eyes, with their changeable color, fascinating. If she wore green, her eyes seemed green. If she had on a blue sweater or shirt, her eyes showed hints of blue. If she wore something dark, the brown highlights revealed themselves.

Her eyes were a lot like Leah herself, Paul decided. Adaptable. Multifaceted.

He'd come to know Leah in the past month. Really *know* her. Appreciate her and her quiet ways. He'd tried to analyze what had happened to him since her arrival in his home, but he couldn't quite figure it out. When she'd first arrived, he'd been consumed with his grief, almost afraid to let go of it. What was left for him if he didn't have his grief? Emptiness? A looming black hole of *nothing*.

After the first week with Leah, he noticed

there'd be periods of time without the harsh pain. He'd feel almost free. Then something would remind him of Diane, of how lonely he was without her, and the pain would return full force. He thought about this new emotional pattern.

Pain.

No pain.

Pain again, but not as intense as before.

Then gone again.

Paul found it curious that Diane's sister could have brought about so dramatic a difference. More curious still that someone who was practically a stranger to him could ease his misery.

He pulled into the driveway of his home, eager to see Leah and the children. Eager to see their progress with the garden. He put his softball mitt in the hall closet and grabbed a cold soda from the refrigerator. He was tasting his first swallow when he happened to look out the sliding glass door.

And froze.

The can was poised in front of his mouth as he watched the scene in the garden. Kelsey was sitting in her stroller, small arms stretched upward, attempting to catch a butterfly. The boys were digging with hand shovels, intent on their task, with Leah looking on, laughing at something one of them said.

The sound of her laughter drifted toward him, and Paul swore he'd never heard anything more beautiful in his life.

She was wearing faded jeans and a short-sleeved green shirt. She'd left the last two buttons unfastened and knotted the tails at her waist. Her hair was caught by the breeze, and the sunshine cast an iridescent glow through the fine strands.

Paul's heart constricted, but not with the pain he was accustomed to feeling. He almost wished it *was* pain. He knew how to deal with that, how to react. But it wasn't pain he felt now.

It was desire.

A desire so gut-wrenching it took his breath away. It wasn't anything as simple as sexual need. He'd never thought of Leah in those terms, never considered making love to anyone other than his wife, who was seven months in the grave. What he was feeling was an emotion totally outside his experience. Bigger than mere desire, bigger than the contentment of companionship or the sharing of grief. Bigger than Leah and him.

Strange as it seemed, he felt an overwhelming urge to sit down and weep. Tears burned for release, tightening his chest, stinging his eyes. With effort he was able to hold them at bay.

Hours later Paul still wasn't sure what it was about that scene that had struck him so hard. Perhaps simply the beauty of those moments. The sky had been bright blue, the sunshine beaming down like God's smile on those he cherished most. His children, who were quietly happy as they scrabbled in the dirt or grasped at butterflies. And Leah . . .

It came to Paul then, as he sat at his desk, looking over some bills and bank statements. He understood now. What had affected him so strongly was . . . life. How glorious life could be. How beautiful. How precious.

For months he'd been in the dark, lingering in the coolness of the shadows. The sudden contrast between light and dark seemed so profound.

When Leah had first come to his house, Paul had been dying. He'd wanted to die with Diane. A month had passed and he'd discovered, much to his surprise, that he wanted to live.

Leah's shoulders ached. She'd spent most of the morning working in the garden with the boys. Not used to that kind of physical exercise, she supposed it was little wonder that her muscles were rebelling. After lunch, she'd taken a long, hot shower and changed her clothes. The boys were tired; they'd gone down for their nap with hardly any complaints.

The house was quiet. Paul was working in his den, the boys and Kelsey were asleep, and Leah settled in a living room chair with her library book. Reading for pleasure was something she'd missed over the past few years. But no more than five minutes into the first chapter, her eyes kept drifting shut.

She woke shortly after three, puzzled to find a blanket draped over her shoulders.

"Good afternoon, Sleeping Beauty," Paul teased when she opened her eyes.

Sitting up, disoriented, Leah glanced around. The last thing she remembered was setting aside her book and resting her eyes. Only for a moment, she'd promised herself.

"The garden looks great," Paul was saying.

Leah's smile was filled with pride. "Thank you. The boys and I worked hard."

"I can tell. They're awake, by the way."

"And hungry, too, no doubt." She began to fold the blanket, ready to get up and meet the demands of her nephews.

"Don't worry about it. We walked down to the store for ice-cream bars. Kelsey went along for the ride."

"Is Leah awake yet?" Ryan asked as he bounded into the living room. He sent her a wide grin when he saw that she was. "Did you tell her about the surprise?" he asked, looking up at his father.

"Not yet."

"What surprise?"

"It's nothing big," Paul explained. "We brought you back an ice-cream bar. I hope you like double fudge."

"I love it. Thank you, Paul." She smiled up at him and, closing her eyes, stretched her arms high above her head and yawned.

When she'd opened her eyes, she saw that he was still watching her. He was frowning, though, which she hadn't seen him do lately. He turned abruptly and hurried into the kitchen.

Leah followed. Ronnie and Ryan dragged a chair over to the fridge and both of them stood on it, squabbling as they opened the freezer. They took out the ice-cream bar they'd bought for her and carried it over to her, each holding one end. Sitting at the table, she opened the small box. The ice cream had melted a little on the walk home.

Paul pulled out a chair, turned it around

and straddled it, resting his arms along the back. "When's the last time you talked to Rob?" he asked unexpectedly.

"Rob?" she repeated, wondering why Paul would ask about him. "I don't know. I haven't thought about it."

"Don't you think it's time the two of you went out?"

"No." Contrary to what Paul seemed to believe, her relationship with Rob didn't involve any real commitment. Which must seem strange to someone like her brother-in-law, who felt so deeply about people and things.

"Shouldn't you call him, then?"

"Not really."

Paul frowned again. "Don't you care about him?"

She shrugged. "Yes, but . . ."

"Then call." He moved off the chair, got one of the portable phones and handed it to her.

"All right, all right," she said with a resigned sigh. She didn't know why it was so important, all of a sudden, for her to call Rob, but in an effort to appease Paul, she'd do it.

As it turned out, Rob sounded pleased to hear from her and suggested they go to a movie that evening. When she mentioned it to Paul, he seemed pleased. More than pleased — relieved.

She found his response odd, but shrugged it off.

"You look nice," he told her when she'd changed for her date several hours later. He was reading the paper, the very one that employed him, when Rob arrived.

Rob, in his mid-forties, had never been what Leah would call her "heartthrob." She doubted that he'd ever been any woman's heartthrob. Tonight he wore a gray cardigan — the same one he'd worn every time they'd gone out, other than to faculty dinners, for the past three years.

Leah introduced the two men. Rob stepped forward and shook Paul's hand, but he seemed a bit nervous, Leah noted, which she hadn't expected.

The boys each wanted a hug, then started to follow her to the door. Paul distracted them and she was able to leave without giving them a chance to ask Rob a lot of questions.

The evening was clear and bright. June weather was generally mild in the Pacific Northwest, and this June was no exception.

"It's good to see you again," Rob said as he helped her into the car. He'd always been a gentleman, and it was the small touches, the old-fashioned manners, that made him so endearing. No one was going to define sex appeal using Rob Mullins as an example, but he was considerate and kind.

"It's good to see you, too," she said with a slight smile.

He walked around the front of the car and joined her in the front seat. "The college seems lonely without you."

"Summer term's pretty slow anyway," she said briskly, not wanting to make too much of his words.

"True, but I always knew you'd be back come fall. It's not going to be the same without you, Leah."

He surprised her by blushing. This was probably the most romantic thing he'd said to her in the three years they'd been seeing each other.

Rob seemed flustered as he inserted the key in the ignition. Leah fastened her seat belt and as Rob backed out of the driveway, a movement in the front window caught Leah's eye.

The twins, grubby hands pressing against the pane, were staring at her. She smiled and waved.

Ryan waved back. Ronnie didn't.

Instead, his thumb went into his mouth.

Leah sighed. Ronnie hardly ever sucked

his thumb these days.

Her eyes were still on the window when Paul appeared, standing behind his sons. His gaze connected with hers, and something indefinable passed between them. The power of that moment left Leah breathless.

Her pulse burst into a rapid-fire speed.

Could it be regret she read in Paul's eyes? That made no sense. Maybe he was only reliving his early carefree days with Diane. Or — maybe — he still felt guilty about interfering with what he persisted in calling Leah's "social life." Anyway, the moment was too brief to be sure of what he might have meant.

What it was, if it was anything at all, Leah couldn't say. By then Rob had driven past the house and the moment was lost.

Leah dropped her gaze to her hands, tightly clenched in her lap. Could it be that Paul *hadn't* wanted her to go out with Rob? That was ridiculous. He'd practically arranged the date himself.

She and Rob had a pleasant enough evening, watching a popular new romantic comedy, but that look she'd exchanged with Paul was never far from her mind.

Although it was shortly after ten when Rob drove her home, the house was dark and quiet.

"Would you like to come in for coffee?" she asked.

"Not tonight, thanks."

Leah hated to admit how grateful she was. They hadn't had much time to talk, thanks to the movie. But although Rob hadn't said much, Leah knew he felt uneasy about her living situation. He didn't ask her any direct questions about Paul, but he'd hinted that he feared something romantic might be developing between Leah and her brother-in-law.

She'd let his insinuations go unanswered. To deny anything would have invited argument. If it hadn't been so completely ludicrous a suggestion, Leah might have laughed.

Paul had loved Diane. Her sister had been beautiful and vivacious; Leah was neither. Diane had been witty and charming; Leah lacked both skills. After loving Diane, there was little chance Paul would ever feel anything more than gratitude for Leah. Deep, heart-felt gratitude, to be sure, but just gratitude nonetheless.

"Could I see you again soon?" Rob asked her, sounding a bit flustered.

"Of course."

"Next week?"

"That would be fine."

76

Rob grinned. "I'll give you a call, then . . . say, Monday evening?"

"I'll be here."

He climbed out of the car and walked around to her side to open the door. He offered her his hand, which she accepted, and escorted her to the front door. Once again he seemed a little ill at ease. Was he planning to kiss her good-night? she wondered. They'd only kissed occasionally. Light kisses. Nothing urgent and certainly nothing close to passionate.

Rob put his arms around her waist and pulled her closer. He gave her the opportunity to object and, when she didn't, he brought his mouth down to hers. It was by far the most ardent kiss they'd ever shared. But Leah had the feeling that he was testing her with it, trying to ascertain whether there was anything romantic between her and Paul.

He broke off the kiss and stared down at her, as if reading her expression.

"Good night, Rob," she said, breaking free of his crushing embrace. "I'll talk to you next week."

Rob released her immediately. "Okay," he said breathlessly. "I'll phone you Monday."

Leah let herself in and, leaning against the door, she sighed. Not with pleasure, but with relief. The movie had been entertaining, and Paul was right — it probably did her good to get away for a few hours. But she hadn't enjoyed herself as much as she'd thought she would.

There hadn't been a lot of opportunity for conversation, of course, but she'd been rather bored with what there was. Rob had seemed — she hated to say it — dull. If he wasn't hinting at a romance between her and Paul, he was making her sound like a martyr for moving in with Paul and the children. It had made Leah uncomfortable.

She saw a sliver of light from under the door to Paul's office and was half-tempted to politely tell him she was home.

Before she could make up her mind, Paul came out.

"I thought I heard you," he said, greeting her with a warm smile. He smiled more often these days, and she marveled at how it changed his whole face — although it never quite seemed to cut through the pain in his eyes.

"I'm home," she announced, feeling slightly nervous and not knowing why.

"How was it?"

"Fine. We went to a movie." She told him which movie they'd seen and added a comment about the lead actors.

Paul nodded and buried his hands in his pockets, striking a relaxed pose. "I'm glad you got out of the house for a few hours."

"You're just feeling guilty about playing softball with your brothers this morning," she said with a slight laugh. "Would you like some coffee? I can make decaf."

"Yeah," he said, following her into the kitchen, "I would."

"Instant okay?"

"Sure."

Leah filled two mugs with water and stuck them in the microwave.

"You should've invited Rob in."

"I did," she said, her back to him as she punched the buttons on the microwave.

"So why didn't he come inside?"

Leah shrugged. "I don't know."

"Because of me?"

"He didn't say." She turned around and folded her arms, waiting for the timer to go off so she could add instant coffee to the hot water.

"You'll be seeing him again, won't you? Soon?"

FOUR

"Yes," Leah confirmed, frowning. It bothered her that Paul seemed so eager to have her out of his home. "Rob and I will be going out again soon."

Paul nodded. "Good idea."

"Good idea?" Leah laughed as she finished stirring decaffeinated instant coffee into the hot water. "Why?" she asked as she handed Paul a mug.

He led the way to the kitchen table and pulled out a chair for her. "It eases my mind."

His answer made no sense to Leah. He must've read the question in her eyes, because he elaborated.

"There's nothing I can do to reimburse you for everything you've done, Leah. I can't afford to pay you."

"Paul . . ."

"I don't own anything valuable enough to give you."

"But Paul —"

"It seems like such a little thing to encourage you to get out every once in a while. I want to be sure you have ample opportunity to do so."

Paul lowered his gaze to his coffee, his hands enclosing the mug.

"It hasn't been so bad." Leah wished she knew of some way to reassure him. Yes, it had taken her a few weeks to work out a schedule for the children, and yes, she was usually exhausted by the end of the day. But she wasn't making some noble sacrifice, as Paul and Rob were implying. Mothering these children was something she *wanted* to do. Already she was reaping rewards beyond anything she'd imagined.

"I want you to have fun," Paul said emphatically.

"Oh, Paul," she breathed. "Don't you think I am? Kelsey, the boys and I had a marvelous time today planting our garden. I'll have those memories all my life. This morning with the children was the most wonderful part of my day — not my date with Rob."

"You should slow down, then," he continued gruffly. "There's no need to keep the house and yard spotless. I feel guilty enough as it is without you working all hours of the day and night."

If Leah had ever heard an exaggeration, this was it. Her housekeeping skills could best be described as adequate. Her interest in planting a garden had come about as the result of a project the boys had brought home from preschool — a seedling inside a Dixie cup. She'd worked hard on the garden, yes, but it was a labor of love.

She couldn't, *wouldn't* slow down. It was partly because of her sense of duty, partly her need to keep busy. Other than summer holidays, this was her first work experience outside a classroom since she was five years old. There was a whole lot for her to learn, to explore.

"I'm enjoying myself."

Paul looked as though he didn't quite believe her.

"I am, honest." She leaned forward and placed her hand on his forearm in an effort to convince him. The action had been instinctive, but the instant her hand touched Paul's arm, Leah realized it was a mistake. She wasn't sure why, except that her heart leapt.

Even hours later, as she lay awake in bed, her mind refused to let go of that moment. She'd removed her hand immediately, and the conversation had continued, but something had changed.

Only Leah didn't know what it was.

She wasn't good when it came to relationships. She'd never been good with them. She recognized love; love was easy. Her feelings toward Kelsey and the twins were as strong as any mother's. Diane might have given birth to the children, but Leah was the one taking care of them now, and her protectiveness toward them was fierce.

In some ways she supposed she loved Paul, too. But on a different level. One that was less clear, less straightforward.

They'd bonded. That was the only logical explanation for what had happened to her when she touched his arm. They'd been through so much together. The trauma of Diane's death. Her funeral. And now the raising of the children. Naturally that had created a bond between them.

This bonding phenomenon, this closeness they now shared, would explain the physical response she'd felt when she touched him. It wasn't a sexual response. Or was it? Leah didn't know. If she'd had more experience with relationships, she might be able to define it better.

Rob had touched her that night, too. His kiss had been probing and urgent. She hadn't liked it, had wanted to rub her lips and erase it when he'd finished.

But with Paul, her senses had leapt to life, and she'd been intimately aware of him. Their eyes had met, and his had stared relentlessly into hers.

Rob had kissed her, and she hadn't felt a fraction of the sensation she had when she'd briefly touched Paul's arm. It was Rob she was dating, though. Rob she'd be spending time with. Rob who'd asked her out.

Now that she had time to think about it, Leah realized she'd prefer it if Rob didn't phone her next week. His insinuations about her and Paul had insulted her. And yet . . . maybe there was some truth to them, although she hardly dared to express it. If it *was* true, that bothered her even more. It just seemed . . . wrong.

Leah felt trapped.

Rob seemed eager to continue their relationship while she felt content without him, satisfied to put everything between them on hold. True, she'd been the one to contact him, but only because Paul had insisted.

It was obviously important to Paul — a matter of pride, even — that she continue to see Rob. As though this was the one thing he could do to ease her load. Nothing she'd said had persuaded him that she was pleased with the status quo.

Her inability to describe her feelings adequately frustrated Leah. For the first time since Diane's death, she felt that her anguish had begun to lift. The children had raised her spirits, returning to her the gift of laughter. It felt so good to wrap her arms around them, to let go of her grief.

Leah smiled to herself in the dark. She hadn't thought of it in those terms before. Being with the children meant she was absorbed by *their* needs. And because she had to consider their feelings ahead of her own, she found herself grieving less. Not that she didn't miss Diane just as much, but that loss no longer felt like an open wound.

Leah couldn't be around the children and continue the melancholy patterns that grief had brought into her life. *She* was the one who'd benefited from coming to live with them. Now if only she could make Paul understand that. . . .

As he'd promised, Rob called Leah Monday evening, right after she'd finished clearing the dinner dishes. Paul answered the phone and, without a word, handed her the receiver. Although he left the kitchen to give her privacy, she couldn't shake the feeling that wherever he was, he'd be able to listen to her side of the conversation.

"Hello, Leah."

"Hi, Rob."

"How are you?"

"Fine, thanks. You?"

"Good."

She wondered if their conversation could get any more banal. "I'm glad to hear it."

"Will you be free Saturday evening?"

"Ah . . . yes. I shouldn't have any problem getting away." Paul would make sure of that.

"Great. What about a poetry reading in Blaine? I know it's a bit of a drive, and we probably won't get back until late, but I think the effort will be worth it."

"That sounds . . . nice." It sounded boring, but Leah didn't feel she had any other option. If she made an excuse, Rob would be convinced there really *was* something between her and Paul. And Paul seemed to find it vitally important that she date Rob.

Leah didn't have a lot of friends. Her best friend had always been her sister, and her only other really close friend, Linda Potter, was traveling in Europe this summer. Getting out with Linda occasionally might have eased Paul's concern, but since she was away, Leah was stuck with Rob.

"Wonderful. I'll pick you up around six, then," Rob said.

86

They spoke for a few more minutes, the same insipid comments that had marked the beginning of the call. Leah hung up, wondering what it was about Rob that had ever interested her. Instinctively she realized they were destined to be no more than casual friends. She also realized it wasn't Rob who'd changed, but her.

No sooner had she ended the conversation than Paul entered the kitchen, his eyes searching hers.

"That was Rob," she explained unnecessarily.

"I gathered as much," he said, revealing no emotion.

"We're going out again on Saturday evening." She didn't have the courage to tell him it was to a poetry reading for fear Paul might laugh, and then she would, too. And laughter between them would be so intimate.

The doorbell chimed just then, and Paul, looking as though he meant to say something else, left to answer it. Leah didn't know if she should be grateful for the interruption or not.

She was arranging the last of the plates in the dishwasher when Elizabeth Manning walked into the kitchen, smiling affectionately when she saw her.

"Hello, Leah."

"Hello!" She greeted Paul's mother warmly, drying her hands on a kitchen towel. Before Diane's death, the Manning parents had been mere acquaintances, but over the past few months Leah had come to love and appreciate them. "When did you get back?"

"This morning."

At the sound of their grandmother's voice, the twins raced out of the back bedroom and hurled themselves at Elizabeth's legs, shrieking with excitement.

Elizabeth laughed and reached down to hug her two grandsons.

Leah smiled at the boys' glee. They'd missed their grandparents. After she'd come to live with Paul, the older Mannings had taken a two-week trip down the Oregon coast in their motor home.

"There's coffee made," Leah said, getting four cups while Elizabeth gave the twins two giant seashells she'd brought back for them. Ryan and Ronnie were thrilled with their gifts. They dragged their grandmother down the hallway to show her the picture of their mother that Leah had put up on the bedroom wall.

When she'd finished pouring the coffee, Leah carried the tray into the living room, where Paul was sitting with his father. He glanced up and smiled at her.

Elizabeth returned with the twins and they all sat down. Elizabeth and Eric were on the couch, with the boys at their feet. Paul was in his recliner and Leah across from him. Kelsey was crawling around on the floor, and after a moment Elizabeth picked her up. Kelsey struggled momentarily, but settled down in Elizabeth's lap to investigate her necklace and then taste it.

"It's good to be home," Eric was saying to Paul. "I suppose we should've phoned first, but we were eager to see how everything was working out for you."

"We're fine, Dad." Paul's eyes drifted to Leah.

It *had* been going well, better than either Paul or Leah had expected. There'd been adjusting on both their parts, but they'd created a comfortable routine. The children were thriving. For a long moment Leah and Paul simply stared at each other.

Leah suddenly realized she needed to say something to break the silence. "Everything is going just great," she confirmed, clearing her throat. She was grateful when Ryan clambered onto her lap. Not wanting to be outdone by his brother, Ronnie joined him. Leah had to peek out from behind the boys' backs. "The twins and I visited the school earlier this week and registered for kindergarten classes."

"We went to the big kids' school," Ryan said eagerly.

"Since the boys have summer birthdays, I was a little concerned about whether they'd be ready for kindergarten," Leah explained.

"But Leah had them tested, and it looks like everything's a go," Paul said, sounding pleased.

"Although I did request the morning session," Leah added. "The boys still need their naps."

"We do not," Ronnie denied righteously. "I'm almost five." He held up his hand, splaying his fingers. Ryan quickly imitated his brother.

"I remember when my boys were that age," Elizabeth said, smiling broadly. "Your daddy felt the same way. 'Five's too old to nap,' he insisted, but I put him down every afternoon because I needed the peace and quiet myself."

"I'm thirty-six years old," Paul said, looking at Leah, eyebrows raised, "and my mother still tells tales about me."

"I always will," Elizabeth told him. "It doesn't matter how old you are, you'll always be my little boy."

Paul's parents left an hour later, after relaying a few of their adventures along the Oregon coast. The visit was a good one.

Leah envied Paul his family. He was close to his siblings and parents. Leah and Diane only had each other. Their mother suffered from a personality disorder, and their father had abandoned the family when the girls were barely old enough to remember him. Leah's grandparents lived on the other side of the country, and she could recall visiting them only once. They'd died while she was in her teens.

Diane had loved Paul's family, too. She'd never complained about problems with her in-laws, and made a point of giving Paul ample opportunity to do things with Jason and Rich, his two younger brothers.

Leah wasn't well acquainted with Paul's siblings, but she knew they'd all pulled together — particularly the boys who, unlike the sisters, lived in Seattle — to help Paul after Diane's death. Paul's pride had stood in the way, and he'd systematically rebuffed their efforts. He'd grudgingly accepted hers, Leah realized, because he'd had no other option.

Things were better now. They'd all begun to adapt. The changes that were taking place in their lives were positive ones and for that,

Leah was grateful.

The following Saturday, Paul was in a foul mood — and he didn't know why. The day had started well, but by evening it had deteriorated. Leah's date had arrived shortly after dinner, and Paul had barely been able to look at the man.

Ryan had wanted ice cream sometime later, and for no reason at all, Paul found himself saying no. The boys had looked shocked when he snapped at them and quickly retreated to their bedroom.

Feeling guilty, Paul had gone in after them, apologized and then together they'd dished up huge bowls of ice cream. The boys had put on their own toppings and smeared chocolate syrup all over the counter. Paul had conscientiously cleaned up the mess.

He didn't want Leah coming home from her night on the town to find the kitchen a disaster.

He thought back over his day, which had been a good one. That further confused Paul. If he'd had to cope with one frustrating event after another, he might be entitled to a foul mood. But he hadn't.

That morning he'd played softball with his brothers. He'd forgotten how much he enjoyed sports, and was disappointed that John Duncan would be returning the next week.

Leah and the kids had surprised him by coming to the park to watch the last couple of innings. It felt great to hear Leah cheering him from the stands. In all the time he'd known his sister-in-law, he'd never heard her raise her voice. He'd played his best when Leah and the kids were there, and afterward, for a treat, he'd taken everyone out to McDonald's.

The afternoon didn't explain his rotten mood, either. He'd repaired the screen in Kelsey's bedroom without a hitch. He'd even had time to mow the lawn. The twins had followed him with their plastic mowers, blowing bubbles into the bright June sunshine.

Leah was in the backyard with Kelsey, planting the herbs she'd picked up at the local nursery. She'd never grown them before and wanted to see how well they did. He'd teased her about having a green thumb, and the sound of her laughter had lingered long after he'd gone into the house.

Before he knew it, dinner was on the table and Leah was getting ready for her date with Rob Mullins. Paul had tried to act nonchalant. He was happy she was going out, wasn't he? Hell, making sure her social life continued was the least he could do. He had to give her a chance to get away from the daily grind of looking after the house and the kids.

Rob seemed like a decent enough guy. A bit on the boring side, but then he hadn't expected a math professor to be a stand-up comedian.

Once the kids were asleep, Paul went into his den and turned on the computer to work on his novel.

He should be thrilled about the opportunity. Overjoyed.

But he wasn't.

His attention span was short, his thoughts on everything but his novel. He worked late, forcing himself to review the five chapters he'd written before Diane's death, making a few changes and corrections as he went.

It was well past eleven when he finished reading. The novel was good. At least he thought it was, but what did he know? Not much, he decided.

He had no reason to delay going to bed, but was strangely reluctant to do so. The boys would be awake before six; he'd told them to crawl into bed with him when they woke up and let Leah sleep.

He checked on the kids, who were sleeping soundly, and glanced at his watch, wondering how much longer Leah would be out. She hadn't told him what time she'd be back, and he hadn't asked. Not that it was any of his business . . .

He sat down in the living room with a novel he'd been wanting to read, but his mind kept wandering. The image of Rob taking Leah in his arms and kissing her sprang, fully formed, into his mind.

Without understanding why, Paul was furious. He slammed the book shut and stood abruptly, his chest heaving with exertion. If Rob was kissing Leah, it had nothing to do with him.

Clenching his fists, he sank back into the chair and opened his book. It didn't make any difference. The anger simmered just below the surface, looking for an excuse to erupt . . . but there wasn't anyone to pick a fight with. Except himself.

He was going to stay awake and wait for her, Paul decided. He didn't care how late she was; he was going to sit right in this chair until she was home. If she didn't come home . . . well, he'd deal with that when the time came. He'd have to do some serious thinking about the situation if it turned out Leah spent the night with Rob Mullins. He didn't want an immoral woman raising his children, he thought heatedly.

Leah? Immoral? *Come on!* Paul wanted to kick himself. He'd never known anyone more forthright and honest.

He heard a car door closing, and his heart went into a panic. He leapt off the chair as if he'd been doing something illegal. If Leah invited Rob inside, he didn't want them to think he was waiting up for her.

Hiding in his bedroom and turning off the lights wouldn't work, either. They would've already noticed the lamp on in the living room.

Thinking quickly, Paul dashed into Kelsey's room. Carefully, so as not to wake her, he scooped her up from the crib and hurried back to his chair, holding his small sleeping daughter in his arms.

He'd been seated no more than a couple of seconds when Leah slipped quietly inside the house. She paused when she saw him and Kelsey, her expression immediately worried.

"Is she sick? I knew I shouldn't have left her when she was teething." The concern in her voice eased Paul's loathsome temper. He glanced down at the slumbering infant. If Kelsey's teeth were bothering her, he hadn't known it. She'd been a perfect baby all evening.

"She's been fussy this week," Leah said, looking guilty. "I'm sorry I —"

"Kelsey's fine . . . now," Paul said, gently placing his daughter against his shoulder and patting her back. He felt like a fool playing this game with Leah — a fool and a jerk — but he didn't have the courage to tell her the truth. "I was just going to put her back to bed."

"Was she up all evening fussing?"

"Not all evening," he said, hating himself for the deception.

"I could use a cup of tea," Leah said, hanging her sweater in the hall closet. "How about you?"

"That sounds good," he answered in a whisper. He carried Kelsey back to her bedroom and put her in the crib.

When he returned to the kitchen, Leah had set the kettle on the burner and was getting two mugs.

She looked lovely this evening, Paul mused, shoving his hands in his pockets as he watched her graceful movements. She looked . . . he searched for the right word. *Beautiful,* he decided. For reasons he couldn't explain, he'd never thought of Leah as beautiful before. She turned to smile at him and he was lost. Lost in her wistfully intriguing smile.

Leah swallowed and glanced away.

Paul shook himself out of his trance and walked to the other side of the kitchen, opening the refrigerator and taking out the milk. He didn't drink his tea with milk, but he needed an excuse to leave her and that one conveniently presented itself.

"I was thinking," he said, setting the milk carton in the center of the table.

"Oh?"

"You should marry Rob." Paul wouldn't have surprised himself more had he suggested they jump off the Tacoma Narrows Bridge together. It was the last thing he wanted. It would be disastrous to the children if Leah left now. Disastrous to him, too.

"Marry Rob?" she echoed, astonished.

"He seems okay." That sounded like faint praise, but he'd sound like a fool if he said the suggestion had been a joke. Given no other option, he took his own stupid idea even further.

"Rob's not the marrying kind," she said.

"Why not?"

She shrugged. "He was married before, and apparently it was a bad experience."

"What about you, Leah?" Paul didn't know why he couldn't leave the subject alone. He didn't know why he felt the need to pursue it again and again, when it was the very thing he dreaded most.

"What *about* me?"

"You should be married." For reasons he couldn't begin to explain, he felt strangely relieved bringing the subject out in the open. He'd never understood why Leah hadn't married. She was generous. Unselfish. She had a sense of humor and she was easygoing — and she loved kids. He'd watched her with the children all these months, and thanked God with every breath he drew that she was there with him.

Leah frowned at his remark. "I guess I'm a lot like Rob. I'm not the marrying kind."

"I don't believe that."

She carried the pot of tea to the table and filled their mugs. Pulling out her chair, she sat down. "I've never been in love."

"Why not?"

Leah laughed. "I don't know. It just never happened."

"How *do* you feel about Rob?"

She shook her head. "I can't see myself in love with him. He's too self-involved. We'll never be anything more than friends."

"Did you have a good time this evening?"

"Fair." She lowered her gaze, and Paul thought he might have detected a blush. "I . . . I don't think I'll be seeing Rob again." She said it as if she expected an argument from him.

"Why not?"

"Because . . . I have my reasons. Do you mind if we discuss something else?"

"Sure, I mean . . . no, I don't mind. I don't mean to pry." Mysteriously, the dark mood that had been weighing down on him all evening suddenly lifted. Paul didn't want to analyze his feelings. He hadn't said anything to Leah earlier, but he wasn't all that impressed with Rob. Asked for specifics, he couldn't have defined his feelings, other than to say he simply didn't feel the other man was right for Leah.

"How'd everything go with the kids tonight?" she asked in a blatant effort to change the subject.

"Good. They all went down without a problem."

"Did Ryan take his blankie to bed with him?"

Paul chuckled. "He made a gallant effort to go without it, but in the end he succumbed."

Leaning back in her chair, Leah took a sip of her tea. "I suspect if Ryan took his blankie to bed with him, then Ronnie figured he had every right to suck his thumb."

"Naturally." Paul smiled and drank his own tea. "I worked on my novel this evening," he said almost shyly. He wasn't sure why he'd even mentioned his book to Leah. He'd given up analyzing the things he said; he only knew it was something he wanted to tell her.

"How's it coming?"

"Better than I thought."

"How far are you into it?"

"Five chapters — a hundred and ten pages, to be exact. I've been doing a bit of revising."

"What's it about?"

Her interest seemed genuine; otherwise Paul wouldn't have bored her with the details. The story had begun to take shape in his mind long before he'd decided to write it down. It was a thriller with an ex-military hero, a reporter heroine and a plot that involved the illegal arms trade, the Russian mafia and the Middle East.

Leah listened intently, then asked him several thought-provoking questions. Paul answered them as best he could, amazed at her insight. Grateful, too, because she'd pointed out a major plot weakness he'd overlooked.

The next time he glanced at his watch it was nearly one. Paul was astonished by that.

They'd been talking for an hour and a half.

"My goodness," Leah said, looking at her own watch. "I had no idea it was so late."

"Me, neither."

They both stood and walked toward the sink. Leah set her cup down first, then Paul followed with his. But when she turned, apparently she didn't realize he was directly behind her. To keep from colliding with him, she jerked back.

Paul's arms instinctively reached out to steady her. His hands closed over her shoulders.

They both froze.

For a long moment neither moved. Paul's eyes drifted slowly over Leah's flushed features. Her arms were raised, her hands braced against his chest. Her breasts —

Stop! Paul chastised himself. He shouldn't be thinking such things. Not about Leah.

"Are you all right?" he asked once he found his voice. He could hardly breathe, hardly think. All he seemed capable of was feeling.

"I'm fine." Her words were scarcely audible, and she was slightly breathless. Her eyes continued to hold his.

Paul knew he should release her. He knew he'd held on to her much longer than necessary. He knew . . . he knew he was going to kiss her.

Before he could stop himself, before his control slipped back into place, Paul lowered his mouth to hers.

FIVE

Paul felt as though someone had carved out his insides. He felt empty . . . no, it wasn't emptiness he was feeling, but he couldn't identify the intense, unfamiliar emotions that raged through him.

He abruptly dropped his arms, letting go of Leah. Wordlessly they stepped away from each other. He saw how swollen her lips were. Her beautiful eyes, more green than brown, were wide and staring up at him.

He wanted to tell her he was sorry, beg her forgiveness, but he couldn't make himself do it. She looked at him unblinking, her face devoid of color.

Then, just as he found the courage to talk to her, she edged her way past him and hurried down the hallway to her bedroom. She closed her door with a resounding bang — which told him how upset she was, otherwise she would never have risked waking the children.

Paul considered going after her, to explain, only he didn't know what he could say that would excuse what he'd done. He waited a few minutes until he could control the trembling in his hands, then turned off the lights and headed down the hallway to his room.

But he hesitated outside Leah's door. Clenching his fists at his sides, he silently berated himself.

He could've stopped himself from kissing her, yet he hadn't. He'd given in to the impulse, knowing full well he'd be faced with regrets later. None of that had mattered at the time. He'd wanted to kiss her. He'd *needed* to kiss her.

He'd pulled her into his arms, touching every inch of her body with his own, adding to his excitement.

Adding to his guilt.

Her right hand had moved from his chest to caress his face. How warm her fingers had felt against his skin. How smooth.

How right.

It was then that he'd deepened the kiss and she'd given a small gasp — Paul didn't know if it was in pleasure or surprise.

Whatever control Paul possessed, which admittedly was darn little, had been lost at that moment. He'd thrust his hands into her hair and hungrily slanted his mouth over hers. Leah's response was undeniable.

He couldn't make himself break away. Couldn't make himself *want* to break away. Her tongue had shyly darted forward, and the kiss became even deeper.

Paul knew he had to end it now. Before they went beyond kissing . . .

He tore his mouth from hers. They were both gasping for breath, their shoulders heaving. The look on Leah's face would haunt him to the grave.

He saw her shock. Her confusion. But what hurt the most was the self-loathing he could see in her eyes. Perhaps it was just a reflection of his own. Paul didn't know anymore.

Defeated, he moved past her bedroom door, taunted by the twin demons of guilt and desire. It hurt to walk away from Leah. It'd been nearly nine months since he'd experienced the ecstacy, the physical release of a woman's body. Nine agonizing, grief-filled months.

But that was no excuse. He wasn't some teenager overwhelmed by hormones. He was fast approaching forty; by now he should have his libido under control.

But was it so wrong to feel again? he asked himself as he readied for bed.

Yes, came the immediate response. When Diane died, he'd known, had accepted, that the sexual part of his life was over. Gone forever. He'd had a healthy, active sex life with Diane, and when she died he couldn't imagine himself ever wanting another woman. He'd felt so certain of that, so sure that being with anyone else would amount to a betrayal of the wife he'd loved.

But perhaps he'd been shortsighted. Perhaps he'd been foolish. He was still alive, after all. He still had needs, desires, the kind a man felt for a woman.

But Leah? His wife's *sister?*

She'd felt so warm. She'd tasted so sweet . . . so womanly.

He felt trapped.

Diane was gone. Dead. He was alive. But was he? He felt caught somewhere between life and death. One foot in the present, the other in the past.

Diane and Leah.

They were sisters. He was *related* to Leah. How could he feel the way he did about her? It was wrong.

A crystal-clear memory of his wife came into his mind. It was the day she'd learned she was pregnant with Kelsey. She'd planned a surprise celebration for when he returned home from work. Leah had taken the boys to the movies, giving him and Diane several uninterrupted hours. They'd made love, then sat up in bed eating ice cream and pickles. The memory of the teasing and the laughter would always stay with him. He'd loved Diane. Loved her more than life itself. But *he* was the one who'd been left behind.

The image of Diane sitting in their bed, ice cream smeared across her mouth, faded. Paul shut his eyes as tightly as he could, trying unsuccessfully to bring her back. Instead it was Leah who drifted into his mind. Leah, crouched in the sunshine as she worked in the garden. The children were gathered around her, Kelsey trying to catch a gold-winged butterfly, his sons busy digging in the dirt.

What had he done? The fact that he'd inflicted himself on Leah filled him with disgust. Heaven only knew what he was going to say to her in the morning.

What *could* he say? He didn't have a single excuse to offer her, not a single explanation to give. Needing her like this, using her like this, had been selfish and wrong.

But it *felt* right, his mind countered. Nothing had ever felt more right.

"No!" he muttered. It was wrong, wrong, wrong.

He was so confused. His thoughts were tangled, contradictory, uncertain.

He didn't know what to do.

Leah couldn't sleep. She lay on her back staring up at the ceiling in the darkened room. Silent tears slipped from the corners of her eyes, rolling into her hair and onto her pillow. She let them fall.

She hadn't known a kiss could be so good. She hadn't known desire could burn so hot. She'd always been sensible when it came to men and relationships. In charge of every situation. Always in control.

Until Paul kissed her. One kiss, and her body had felt as if it were on fire.

Her heart was still beating much too fast, its cadence echoing in her ear. Her body throbbed with pleasure.

With shame.

With need.

If only Paul had said something. But she'd seen the stricken look in his eyes, seen for herself his tortured regret. His reaction had hurt her more than anything since Diane's death. Unable to bear it, Leah had turned, with as much dignity as she could muster, and retreated to her bedroom.

But her dignity was cold comfort.

If only she understood what had prompted

Paul to kiss her. Had she, without realizing it, done or said something to lead him on, sent inadvertent messages, seeking his touch?

She must have; otherwise, she wouldn't have gone so eagerly into his arms. Otherwise, she would've broken away. It was all too clear how willingly she'd accepted his embrace.

Mortified by the thought, she covered her hot face with both hands.

Shivering, Leah remembered the blatant way she'd responded to him. She'd opened up to Paul. Opened her arms. Opened her heart. And . . . her face grew hotter still. She'd been looking for more. Much more.

She'd lost herself in his kiss, responding to him as she never had to any other man. She'd actually pressed herself against him. . . .

The kiss had gone wild, and demand had shot through her veins. For the first time in her life, Leah had felt completely out of control with a man. She'd wanted him so badly. Wanted to feel his arms around her. Wanted his kiss. Wanted to experience the welcoming touch of his tongue . . .

She'd wanted her sister's husband.

Leah closed her eyes and waited for revulsion to attack her. Waited for guilt to bury her.

She waited. And waited.

But it didn't come. Not the revulsion or the guilt.

Yet in her heart of hearts, Leah experienced such regret it all but consumed her. Regret because of the way he obviously felt about their kiss. It seemed to her that *he* was feeling the revulsion and guilt she wasn't. That, too, was a painful reality — Paul's disdain for her because of what they'd done. What *she'd* done.

Was she falling in love with him? Leah asked herself.

She couldn't answer that any more than she could answer any of the other questions that tormented her.

Her fingers touched her still-swollen lips. They felt bruised — just like her heart. The memory of that moment in his arms returned, bringing with it all the fever, all the madness, all the fury, of their kiss.

She shouldn't be feeling these things, she chastised herself. It was wrong.

How was she going to look Paul in the eye the next morning? How was she going to pretend nothing had happened?

Around her the night breathed. The dark closed in. The rain, which had been threatening all evening, tapped against the windows.

It was a long time before she fell asleep.

Leah woke the next morning, feeling as though she hadn't slept at all. The boys were awake; she could hear them in the kitchen. Apparently Kelsey was up, as well. She turned onto her side and glanced at her clock radio. It was nearly nine. How Paul had been able to keep the kids from waking her was a mystery. Throwing back the covers, she got out of bed and quickly dressed for church.

"Leah," Ronnie cried when she walked into the kitchen, "Ryan got the prize in the cereal box. Tell Daddy it's my turn!"

"I don't remember whose turn it is," she told him, surprised to see that the boys and Kelsey were already dressed.

"It is so my turn," Ronnie insisted.

"Ryan can share." Paul's gruff voice didn't make her feel any better. So far Leah had been able to avoid looking at him, but she wouldn't be able to keep that up for much longer.

He hadn't spoken directly to her, which did nothing to ease the tension between them. Leah could feel the strained nervousness as intensely as she'd felt his touch the night before.

She poured herself a cup of coffee and hurried into the bathroom, where she applied her makeup. By the time she'd finished, Paul had set the breakfast dishes in the dishwasher and wiped the table.

Leah half expected him to make an excuse to skip church that morning. She was half hoping he would. But apparently he didn't plan to stay home, much as she would've preferred it.

They didn't exchange a word on the short drive to the church. Even the children were strangely quiet.

Once they arrived, Leah brought Kelsey to the nursery, while Paul escorted the boys to their Sunday school class.

When Leah entered the church, she saw that Paul's parents had arrived and, sighing with relief, went to sit with them. Rich and Jamie sat in the pew directly in front of Eric and Elizabeth. Being surrounded by Paul's family comforted Leah, made her feel welcome and accepted.

As Paul slipped into the seat next to her, she noticed that he maintained a safe distance between them.

The service passed in a blur for Leah. Her head was so full of what had happened between her and Paul, she couldn't concentrate on the sermon.

When they stood for the closing hymn, Elizabeth Manning leaned toward Leah and whispered, "Are you feeling all right?"

Leah quickly nodded.

"You're looking pale." She paused. "So is Paul."

"I'm fine." But Leah's heart was hammering. She was a little taken aback by how easily Elizabeth had detected the tension between her and Paul. She could only pray that her alarm didn't show in her eyes.

As they finished singing the final verse of the hymn, Leah felt Paul's gaze. Everything in her wanted to turn and look at him, but she lacked the courage. Eventually they'd need to speak to each other. Eventually they'd have to discuss what had happened. But she wasn't ready now and she didn't know how long it would take before she was.

Leah met Jamie, Rich's wife, on her way into the nursery to pick up Kelsey. "You're coming, aren't you?" she asked. At Leah's blank look, Jamie elaborated. "Mom wants all of us to come over for brunch. Paul must've forgotten to tell you."

"Ah . . ."

"Typical man," Jamie said with a smile. "How's everything working out?"

"Great," Leah responded with a too-bright

smile. She'd only talked to Paul's sister-in-law a handful of times, but she liked Jamie. Bethany, Jamie and Rich's little girl, was nearly eighteen months old and, from something Paul had said, it looked as if the couple would be having a second child soon.

Paul met Leah in the hallway outside the nursery. "Mom and Dad invited us to brunch," he said brusquely. "Is that all right with you?"

"It's fine."

These were the first words they'd spoken all morning.

"If you'd rather, I could drop you off at the house and take the kids over myself."

The suggestion hurt — he was trying to avoid her — but she tried not to let it show. "It'd . . . only raise questions if I didn't come."

"You're sure?"

She shifted a squirming Kelsey in her arms. "If you'd prefer me not to be there, just say so." Her eyes defiantly met his.

"I want you there," he admitted, then turned and left her.

In retrospect Leah realized she should've taken Paul up on his offer to drop her off at the house. The brunch at his parents' was trying for both of them. Although they'd attempted to disguise the tension, Leah knew they hadn't succeeded.

After she and Paul had gathered up the kids, Eric and Elizabeth walked them out to the car. They didn't say anything; they didn't have to. Their concern was all-too-apparent in their worried expressions and the lack of conversation.

All three children fell asleep in the car on the ride home. Leah carried Kelsey, while Paul dealt with the boys. She was on her way out of the baby's room, headed to her own room for a nap, when Paul stopped her.

"We have to talk," he said starkly.

Leah nervously shifted her weight from one foot to the other, her heart pounding with dread. She wasn't ready for this. Yet she knew they couldn't delay a confrontation much longer.

"I'm not sure where to start," he said after an awkward moment.

Leah said nothing. She didn't know where to start, either. But she felt a heady sense of relief that he was willing to bring everything out into the open.

"I didn't mean for it to happen," he said, his anger close to the surface. "I certainly didn't plan it."

"I . . . realize that."

"I know I frightened you."

"No." She couldn't very well tell him that

their kissing was one of the most beautiful experiences of her life. She couldn't admit that she'd never felt in any man's arms the things she had with him.

"I didn't?" He seemed surprised to learn that. He hesitated, then turned abruptly and moved away from her. "I . . . I don't know what came over me. I love Diane . . . I haven't been with a woman since . . ."

At the mention of her sister's name, Leah went stiff. The implication nearly choked her. "In other words, I just happened to be handy."

"No!" he practically shouted. "That wasn't it at all."

"Then what was it?"

"If I knew that, do you think I'd be putting us through this hell?" he demanded. "I didn't kiss just any woman. It was you. I'm attracted to *you,* Leah." It sounded as though he was confessing to some particularly shameful crime. "I have no idea when it happened, or even how. I suspect it's only natural, the two of us living together under one roof."

"I don't buy that."

"Why not? I'm being as honest and as objective as I can."

"I know," she breathed softly.

"Then what don't you buy?"

117

When it came right down to it, Leah couldn't believe that Paul could possibly find her attractive after having loved Diane. Leah knew her own skills and assets, and captivating men wasn't one of them. She'd discovered early in life that she couldn't compete with her sister. She hadn't wanted to. She'd loved Diane.

Paul had loved Diane, too. And having loved a woman who was laughter and sunshine and beauty, it wasn't likely he'd be interested in one who was sensible and plain and dull.

But she couldn't find the words to explain this to Paul. The uncomfortable silence grew.

"I . . . think it might be best if we both put the incident behind us," she finally said.

"That doesn't answer my question."

"I don't want to talk about it," she insisted, raising her voice.

Her fervor seemed to surprise him. "So you'd rather forget it ever happened?"

"Yes."

He eyed her skeptically. "Can you?"

"Yes," she lied. "Can't you?"

He hesitated, then nodded. "And it goes without saying that it won't happen again. You have my word on it."

■ ■ ■ ■

Paul knew he'd blundered badly in his conversation with Leah. Seeing her that morning, watching the way her eyes avoided his, was agonizing. He wanted to take her hands in his and plead for her forgiveness. But when he'd built up the courage to confront her, he'd done it all wrong. He'd made it seem as if he'd kissed her because he'd gone nearly a year without sexual gratification and she was available.

He hadn't even told her how sorry he was.

But was he?

Paul didn't know anymore. He'd woken and his arms felt empty without her. For long seconds he lay there, his heart racing.

He waited for the guilt to kick him in the teeth. For Diane's image to appear and damn him for his weakness. For God to intervene and save him from himself.

It didn't happen.

All he could think about was how much he wanted to kiss Leah again.

Her reaction in the morning had quickly convinced him that his actions had betrayed a basic trust between them. She was embarrassed, perhaps even frightened. He'd known that he'd need to reassure her. He should've done it immediately, as soon as she'd entered the kitchen. But he'd waited, telling himself he'd do it right after church. Then they'd ended up at his parents' house, and that second delay had only made it more difficult.

During the ride home he'd rehearsed what he planned to say. It had sounded good in his mind, but the minute he'd tried to voice his thoughts, he'd botched everything.

What else could he do but promise never to touch her again? It was obvious that he'd offended her. His need had repulsed her.

Leah napped well into the afternoon. When she woke, Paul was in his den, presumably working on his novel. He didn't come out until dinnertime, and then only long enough to eat before he returned to his private refuge.

After their baths Leah read to the boys until they were sleepy and her voice had grown hoarse. Once the kids were tucked in their beds, she withdrew into her room and read late into the night.

By the time she woke in the morning, Paul had already left for the office.

The boys requested Eggs McManning for breakfast. By now Leah was quite proficient at creating the family favorite. She was standing in front of the stove, the spatula in her hand, when her eyes suddenly filled with tears. They came so unexpectedly that she was caught completely unawares. She brushed them with her forearm, hoping the twins wouldn't notice.

Why was she weeping, anyway? Was it because she was falling in love with a man who could never love her back? Because she lay awake nights remembering how hot and urgent his mouth had felt on her own? Because she dared not look him in the eye for fear he'd know what she wanted?

There was an even more pressing question: How could she go on, living in his house, caring for his children, as if everything was still the same?

Paul let himself in the house and was immediately met by the enticing aroma of dinner. He walked unnoticed into the kitchen and stopped, mesmerized by the sight of Leah at the stove. He'd purposely avoided her that morning, left early just so he wouldn't have to smile and pretend nothing had changed between them. He'd never been much good at pretending; his expertise was in escape, which was why he'd gone to work early. Now he doubted the wisdom of his actions.

The impact of seeing Leah, of being this close to her after nearly twenty-four hours, hit him hard. It was like being punched in the chest, his lungs emptied of air.

He must've made some kind of noise because Leah turned to face him. "I didn't hear you come in," she said, sounding as normal as always.

Paul was slowly going out of his mind, and there she stood, frying pork chops as if nothing was wrong. He had to marvel at her ability to pretend. To him, the tension was thick enough to slice into bite-sized pieces.

But . . . maybe it was all him. Maybe she *didn't* feel it. Maybe he was the only one.

That thought, somehow, wasn't comforting.

Paul didn't realize his mistake until they were finished with dinner. Leah had said very little. She'd been careful not to look at him even when he asked her a question, which she'd made a point of answering as tersely as possible. The boys were cranky; Paul blamed it on the tension between him and Leah — a tension that proved her emotions were no less involved than his. She'd almost fooled him, though, almost convinced him. She'd certainly given a performance worthy of an Academy Award.

Yet he said nothing. How could he? Like her, he was trapped. He had to continue pretending.

It rained again that night, beating against his window in a relentless rhythm. For the third night in a row, Paul found it difficult to sleep. The howling wind wasn't helping.

He considered getting up, drinking a glass of milk. Maybe reading for a while. Of course, he could revert to pacing away the long hours until morning, the way he'd done the first few months after Diane's death.

What really kept him awake was Leah. Knowing she was so close. Only two doors away . . .

Night. Wind. Rain. Wanting Leah. Loving Diane. Suddenly it was all too much for him, and he tossed aside the blankets and climbed out of bed. Bare-chested, he walked into the kitchen and opened the refrigerator to pour himself a glass of milk, which he gulped down. Rinsing out the glass, he set it in the sink, then headed back to his room.

A movement in the shadows startled him.

"Leah?"

"Paul?"

"What are you doing up?"

"I — I couldn't sleep. I was just going to get myself some milk."

His eyes quickly adjusted to the dark. As soon as they did, Paul wished they hadn't. She stood in the shadows, but the pale light coming from the night-light in the twins' bedroom silhouetted her slight form, highlighting her breasts and the slimness of her waist and hips. He already knew how she felt in his arms and — Paul shook his head and nearly groaned out loud as he deliberately chased the memory from his mind.

"Why are you up?" she asked breathlessly.

"I couldn't sleep, either." His heart was pounding so hard he was afraid she could hear it.

The silence lingered, grew embarrassingly long, yet neither moved.

"I . . . had a glass of milk, too," he offered when the silence seemed to stretch to the breaking point. He was surprised by how difficult it was to speak coherently.

The desire to touch her was suddenly so strong he had to clasp his hands behind him in order to resist reaching for her.

"The storm . . . kept me awake." Leah's voice was barely a whisper. She looked up at him, her eyes wide and imploring.

Waiting. Wanting.

Still neither of them moved. Neither breathed.

Paul groaned inwardly. Wasn't she aware

of the signals she was sending him?

Apparently not. His control was almost at its end. But he held on to it, because the truth was, he suspected she didn't actually know what she was doing, staring up at him like that.

"I should be getting back to bed," he muttered.

"Yes."

They were so close her breath fanned his face. Then Leah lifted her head and their lips were mere inches apart. Their breathing was erratic, and he shut his eyes, concentrating on her scent, relishing the feel of her breath on his face.

"Leah . . ." His voice came from deep within his throat. "Stop me," he groaned.

He was seconds away from taking her in his arms and breaking his promise to himself. His promise to the memory of his dead wife, his promise to God, but most important, his promise to Leah.

Six

Paul didn't know how he managed to avoid kissing Leah. He stumbled back to his room and literally fell across his bed. He heard her return to her bedroom, and only then was he able to breathe easily.

He'd expected to encounter all kinds of problems when Leah moved in with him and the children, but this wasn't one of them. Having to fight a sexual attraction to her hadn't once entered his mind.

Who would've believed this could happen? Not Paul.

It had all started with a simple kiss. An anything-but-simple kiss, he amended. He would gladly surrender everything he owned not to have touched her that first time. Not to have tasted her sweetness, felt her willingness.

One kiss had brought him past the point of pleasure; it had opened a Pandora's box of hungry need.

126

His desire for her was shameless. Just a few minutes ago, it had taken all the control he possessed to walk away from her. He wasn't sure he'd have the strength to do it again.

Where did that leave them?

Paul couldn't explain what had come over him the past few days. Although he was nearly thirty when he married Diane, he hadn't had an extensive history of sexual experience. His army buddies had bragged about their sexual conquests and playfully joked with Paul, claiming he was the only man they knew who was more interested in a woman's mind than her body.

Not with Leah. He'd been fighting erotic fantasies about her for days, doggedly pushing them out of his mind and then damning himself for his thoughts.

For years he'd prided himself on his self-control, his discipline, but lately that discipline was breaking down. In fact, it was going to hell in a hand basket, as the saying went.

Although his breathing calmed, the frightening excitement didn't lessen once Paul was in his own room; if anything, it increased. Every time he closed his eyes, Leah was there, looking up at him, her beautiful eyes languid with desire. Every instinct he had told him to take her in his arms and hold her tight. He longed to curve his hands around her waist and nestle close to her softness.

What was he going to do? He'd already discovered he couldn't ignore her. He couldn't be in the same room and not react to the tension between them. No matter how hard he tried, he couldn't keep the memories of the night he'd kissed her from bombarding his mind. No more than he could repress the guilt those same memories occasioned.

Paul didn't know how Leah managed to pretend that this strained awareness didn't exist. She did a masterful job of it, but that ability was beyond him.

He could do what he'd done that morning — leave for work early in order to avoid any contact, verbal or otherwise, with Leah. But the problem with that was his children. He couldn't escape her without depriving himself of what little time he had with them. In the end he'd only be cheating himself.

The one other option that presented itself was an open, honest discussion. However, he'd attempted that once and made a mess of it.

Paul sighed wearily. The situation was even worse than he'd thought. Quite simply, he had no idea what to do now.

"Your parents phoned." That was how Leah greeted Paul when he returned home from work the next evening. Just the way she said it told him she'd had a bad day. He was almost glad. His own had been a disaster, and if she was miserable, too, he figured that was only fair.

His mood lightened considerably.

"What's up with them?"

Leah shrugged, keeping her back to him — an irritating habit of late. "They asked if they could come visit."

"What did you tell them?"

Hearing his father, Ryan ran in from the backyard, and Paul lifted his son into his arms, hugging him briefly.

"What *could* I say?" Leah continued, turning to face him. "I told them they were welcome anytime."

Ronnie raced in behind his brother, looking for the customary hug. Paul absently complied, then bent over and kissed Kelsey's cheek as she gleefully pounded away on a pan with a wooden spoon.

"They wanted to be sure we were both going to be home."

Paul straightened slowly. "That sounds ominous."

"I . . . think it might be." Leah turned back to the counter, where she was grating cheese for a taco salad.

Paul reached over and stole a black olive from the bowl of lettuce. "Why do you say that?"

"I know your mother sensed something was wrong . . . between us Sunday morning," she explained.

"So?" Paul was surprised that he could act so nonchalant, since he felt anything but. Not that he was worried about his parents' visit, of course. No reason he should be.

"So . . . it worries me."

"Why?"

She whirled around and glared at him, and it was all Paul could do not to clap his hands and cry out, "Hot damn!" Finally. Finally. Leah Baker was showing some emotion. She couldn't pretend anymore. She couldn't ignore him any longer. Couldn't continue this maddening game of make-believe.

His parents arrived at seven-thirty. The kitchen was clean, and the boys were outside playing on the swing set in the still-bright sun. Kelsey had been diapered and put to bed for the night. Paul had to marvel, not for the first time, at Leah's efficiency.

The minute his father stepped into the house, his gaze sought out Paul's. There was something on his mind, all right. Paul knew the look. The last time Paul could remember seeing that particular expression was when Christy had announced she was married to Cody Franklin. The news came as a shock, especially since she'd been engaged to James Wilkens at the time. Leave it to his youngest sister to marry one man while engaged to another.

"So, what's bothering you, Dad?" Paul asked.

"I'd like to talk to you."

"Sure."

Eric sent Leah an apologetic look. "Privately, if you don't mind?"

"Of course not." Paul sent Leah a glance, too. Her eyes met his, and she looked so uncertain, so dubious, that he had to resist an urge to tell her there was nothing to worry about. But he didn't say anything, because he wasn't sure himself.

"And while you two are chatting, Leah and I can have some time to ourselves," his mother said conversationally. Except that Paul wasn't fooled. He recognized her concerned tone of voice. When he was a teenager, that concern had often led to having the car keys taken away, or being grounded — until he saw things the same way his parents did.

Whatever was going on seemed worrisome. Leah, who'd apparently recovered, cast him a prim I-told-you-so look and led his mother into the kitchen.

Whatever this was all about, Paul was pretty sure he didn't like it. His parents were wonderful; the first six months after Kelsey was born, Paul couldn't have survived without their encouragement and support. But he was thirty-six years old, far past the point of being reprimanded by them.

Leah claimed his parents had sensed that things had gone awry, although Paul doubted it. Yes, the mood had been a bit tense and his family might've read something into it, but surely that hadn't brought about this unexpected visit.

Paul preceded his father into his office and closed the door. The room wasn't large, but adequate for his needs. The desk, with his computer, took up one wall. Two more walls were dominated by bookshelves. Paul gave his father the desk chair and took the stool for himself.

"What's wrong, Dad?"

"Nothing." As he spoke, he slowly raised

his eyes to meet Paul's. "At least I hope not."

Paul smiled benignly and waited.

"As you know, your mother and I are leaving next week for Montana. She's got her heart set on being with Christy for the birth of this baby."

"Yes, I know. You don't need to worry about the house. Jason, Rich and I will look after the old homestead for you."

"It's not the house I'm worried about," Eric said gruffly.

"Then what is it?"

"It's Leah."

Paul went stiff. So much for all the reassuring things he'd been telling himself. His father was staring at him as though he expected Paul to leap up and announce that he was lusting after Leah. Not that it was exactly a lie.

"What about Leah?" Paul asked once he could trust his voice not to betray his uneasiness.

"I'm concerned about her."

There was no question that Leah worked too hard and didn't take enough time for herself. Diane had been far more social than Leah, more outgoing. Leah's idea of indulging herself was reading a good book.

"The family realizes that everything's on

the up-and-up between you two."

"On the up-and-up?"

"That the two of you aren't sleeping together," Eric explained bluntly.

His father was entering territory Paul considered off limits. "Dad, listen, I know you mean well, but I don't think —"

"Paul, I hate to broach the subject, but there've been rumors. It's only natural, I suppose. I'm well aware that men and women live together without benefit of marriage all the time. Sadly it's a matter of course these days."

"Dad, I don't care what other people think." There'd always be those who believed whatever they wanted to, no matter how innocent the situation.

His father folded his arms over his chest and nodded. "Perhaps not, but how does Leah feel?"

Paul was stunned. He hadn't given Leah's reputation a moment's thought. She was the one who'd suggested moving in with him, after all. He'd assumed, perhaps erroneously, that whatever talk there was didn't concern her. Now, imagining anyone daring to criticize Leah sent hot fury racing through his veins. He wasn't a man to get angry often, but he was now.

"Who's been gossiping about us?" he

134

demanded of his father. "What did they say?"

"That's not important."

"The hell it isn't! I want to know who —"

"There are a few other, more important issues you should be considering," his father interrupted.

That worried Paul even more. Had the rumors turned vicious? "Such as?"

"When Leah moved in with you — it's been what? Six, seven weeks?"

He nodded brusquely. Her coming had changed his life. For the first time in nearly a year Paul wasn't suffocating under the burden of emotional pain, suffocating under the strain of nurturing his children alone. Leah had provided much more than child care, though. She'd cheered his grief-stricken heart, given him a reason to wake up every morning, brought him into the sunlight.

"What about her health insurance?"

"Her health insurance?" Paul exploded. First his father said Leah's reputation was on the line and now he was worried about her health insurance.

"When you said she'd be moving in with you for the next couple of years, I wondered," his father continued. "From what I understand, the college benefit program will only carry her for a few more months and then she'll be canceled. In this day and age, no one can risk going without medical insurance."

"I . . . hadn't thought of that." Now that he'd simmered down, Paul felt like a selfish jerk. He'd never bothered to ask Leah about her medical coverage. He'd been so grateful for her help he hadn't stopped to fully consider the cost of her sacrifice.

"What about her other benefits? Will she be losing those, as well?"

"I don't know."

"While we're discussing Leah, let me bring up something else. Have you had your will altered?" his father asked.

"My . . . will?"

"Your legal affairs need to be in order, son. If anything were to happen to you now, what would become of the children? With Diane gone, they could be made wards of the state unless there's some provision for them in your will."

Paul was stunned by his lack of foresight. "I didn't realize." He slowly expelled his breath and rubbed a weary hand down his face. "I'll make an appointment with James first thing in the morning." Although Christy had broken her engagement with James Wilkens, the attorney remained a good family friend.

"You need to do more than that," his father said emphatically.

"I do?" Paul could only guess at what else he'd let slide.

Eric Manning hesitated. It wasn't often Paul saw indecision in his father's face. "You might not like what I'm about to say. You can tell me it's none of my business, and you'd be right, but since you asked, I'm going to tell you. I think you should marry Leah. The sooner the better."

"Would you like some iced tea?" Leah asked Paul's mother, trying to disguise her nervousness.

The sliding glass door to the backyard was open, and she kept her eye on the twins. Only that morning she'd found them weeding the garden; unfortunately they'd yanked up all the herbs she'd planted with such care.

"No, thank you, my dear." Elizabeth pulled out a kitchen chair and sat down.

Elizabeth lowered her eyes to her hands, folded atop the table, as though she, too, felt on edge. "I've been meaning to have this talk with you for some time, Leah. I probably shouldn't have waited this long."

Leah's heart seemed to stop. Paul's

mother *knew.* As hard as Leah had struggled to hide it, Elizabeth had read the love in her eyes. And if she'd recognized that, then surely she'd seen the guilt and the confusion.

Leah sank into the chair across from Paul's mother. It was all she could do not to cry out that she'd never meant for Paul to kiss her.

"Our family is deeply indebted to you, Leah," his mother began.

"Nonsense."

"No," Elizabeth said firmly. "We're grateful for the way you've stepped in and helped Paul and the children. You've made a world of difference to their lives, and ours, too.

"I was terribly worried about Paul after Diane died, you know. I thought he might need counselling, but he gradually worked through his grief."

"We both have." Learning to deal with her sister's death had been a painful process for Leah, too.

"The twins are doing so much better," Elizabeth went on. "You were right, they needed their own home and their own toys and familiar friends. These last two months have been good for Ryan and Ronnie. There's color in their cheeks and they're laughing again. And Kelsey's growing like a weed."

"I found her standing up this morning. That little rascal's going to be walking soon." Leah had difficulty keeping the pride out of her voice.

Elizabeth beamed. "That's a perfect example of what I mean."

"You give me more credit than I deserve."

"I doubt it." Elizabeth's smile slowly faded, and her blue eyes grew serious. "I believe you told Paul you'd be willing to stay with him and the children until the boys were in school full-time and Kelsey's in preschool?"

Leah nodded. "He won't have to deal with three preschoolers a couple of years down the road. By then, he'll be able to deal with the situation a lot better."

"What do you think will happen to the children after you leave?" Elizabeth asked candidly.

"I — I don't understand."

"How do you think the twins and Kelsey will react once you move out?" she elaborated.

"That's several years away. There's no way of knowing how they'll feel."

"I think there is. The twins have already lost their mother, and we're both aware of how deeply Diane's death affected them."

Leah said nothing, her heart growing heavy with doubts.

"As for Kelsey . . . you're the only mother she's ever known."

"Oh, dear," Leah breathed. "I never thought . . . I just didn't realize . . ." She'd been so stupid, so blind. She'd hoped her moving in with Paul would be a solution; instead it was creating more problems. The time would come when she'd have to go. She couldn't continue living with Paul indefinitely.

"What should I do?" she asked, her eyes pleading with Paul's mother. "I can't leave the children now — I love them so much." A panicky feeling washed over her. She'd been foolish and thoughtless, but it was too late to change that now.

"I know how you feel about the children."

That was something else Leah had failed to consider — her own feelings. She loved these children as much as if she'd given birth to them herself. Walking away from them would be agony — unbearable agony.

"There *is* a solution." Elizabeth's voice came through the haze of regrets in Leah's mind. "Although you may not completely agree with me . . ."

Leah raised her eyes to Elizabeth's, her

heart in turmoil. "Solution?" she whispered.

"Leah, I've upset you."

"No . . . no." She reached for Elizabeth's hands. "You've pointed out some things I should've considered. I can't believe I was so . . . thoughtless."

Elizabeth nodded and, looking a bit uneasy, asked, "I hope you won't feel I'm prying — but how's your relationship with Paul?"

Leah could feel the color rise to her cheeks. "We get along . . . just fine. We always have. He's wonderful with the children, and I've always liked and respected him." She knew she was talking too fast, but couldn't make herself slow down.

"So, the two of you are compatible?"

"Oh, yes — we haven't had a single disagreement." She didn't think she could count a kiss as a dispute. Perhaps if they were at odds more often, she wouldn't feel this growing attraction to him.

"I hear from Paul that you're dating a fellow professor."

"Sort of . . . yes. His name's Rob Mullins, and we've gone out a couple of times in the last few weeks." She didn't mention that she wouldn't be seeing Rob again.

Elizabeth hesitated, and Leah had the impression she found this part of the conversation disconcerting. "Do you have . . . feelings for Rob?"

Leah frowned, not sure where Elizabeth was going with this. "Not exactly — we're friends."

Elizabeth seemed relieved at that. Her smile broadened, and she gently squeezed Leah's fingers. "As I said earlier, I think Eric and I may have come across the perfect solution. We talked about it at some length and although we're well aware that what happens between you and Paul is none of our concern, we felt we needed to speak up."

"Of course."

Elizabeth made a shallow attempt at a smile. "Have you ever thought of marrying Paul?"

Marrying Paul?

For some reason Leah recalled the night before, when she'd been unable to sleep and had left her room, hoping a glass of milk would help. She hadn't known Paul was up. If she had, she would never have ventured into the hallway. Would never have opened her door.

By the time she noticed her mistake, it was too late. Although she'd plastered herself against the wall in the hallway, willing him to pass and return to his own room, he'd stayed where he was, his eyes meeting hers in the dim light.

Before she could stop herself, Leah had realized they were only inches apart. She'd so desperately wanted his touch that she'd nearly swayed into his arms.

How they were able to break away from each other Leah didn't know. She hadn't realized it was possible for two people to come so close to making love without even touching.

"Leah?" Elizabeth's voice broke into her thoughts.

"Yes?" Startled, she looked up, surprised to find that Paul and his father were in the room.

"I believe we've given these two something to think about," Eric Manning was saying. "We should leave now and let them discuss it in privacy."

Elizabeth stood and Leah did, too, impulsively hugging Paul's mother. She closed her eyes for a moment, wondering how to rectify what she'd done. These past few weeks had been among the happiest of her life. For the first time since childhood, she felt as though she belonged, as though she was needed and loved. But in her ignorance she'd overlooked what should've been obvious. Worse, she didn't know what to do about it. Elizabeth's suggestion would never work. Paul wouldn't want to marry her. Nor should he have to.

Paul and his father exchanged handshakes, and then Paul escorted his parents to the front door. Leah set her iced tea glass in the sink.

When he returned to the kitchen, Leah was staring down at the kitchen table. Then, seeking his reassurance, she slowly raised her eyes to his.

"Tell me about your health insurance!" Paul said, sounding angry.

"My . . . health insurance?"

"Yes." It was so rare for Paul to raise his voice that he'd shocked her.

"I could be ruining the children's lives, and you're worried about my *health insurance?*"

"What?" He shook his head. "You've been canceled, haven't you?" he demanded.

Leah shrank from the cold fury she saw in him. "I don't know. . . . Is it important?"

"Yes. And what did you mean you've 'ruined the children's lives'? You've been our salvation!" He rammed both hands through his hair. "I'm the one who's been selfish." He walked away from her, then pivoted sharply. "Why didn't you say something?"

144

"About my health insurance? Trust me, Paul, I was dealing with more important matters."

"Like planting a garden?"

"Yes, like planting a garden." She didn't understand his anger. It was so unlike him. She turned away, fighting tears. "If it'll make you happy, I'll see to it tomorrow morning. Why are you acting like this?"

"My father pointed out a few home truths." He grimaced. "I can't believe I've been so obtuse. I should never have allowed you to move in."

Leah thought she might be physically sick. Paul was going to send her away. For all the reasons his mother had mentioned.

"No!" Her cry came straight from her heart. "I won't let you do it."

"Do *what?*"

"Send me away. I'll fight you. I'll even fight your parents, but I refuse to leave Kelsey and the twins." *And you,* she added silently.

"Send you away?" Paul repeated, aghast. "I shouldn't have let you come, but now that you're here, I'd never make you go. . . ." He hesitated, suddenly pale. "Unless that's what you want."

Tears of release and relief filled her eyes. She brushed them aside, not wanting Paul to know how badly she'd needed his assurance.

"Do you *want* to leave, Leah?"

She glared at him, her eyes defiant. "No! I just got done telling you that."

He sighed and took one step toward her, then stopped, his look intense. "Did my mother suggest the same solution to you as my dad did to me?"

Leah watched him closely, hoping to read his reaction. "She . . . thought we should get married."

"And?"

"And . . . I haven't had time to think about it. But it seems . . . above and beyond the call of duty for you to marry me."

Paul's eyes narrowed as he studied her. Apparently he didn't understand.

"I already explained I'm not the marrying kind," she added, trying to salvage what remained of her pride.

"I never have understood that attitude. You're a warm, gracious, generous woman. What makes you think you're unmarriageable?"

Leah laughed nervously. She'd never received much attention from the opposite sex, not even when she was younger and prettier. She was too bookish for most men. Too serious. She hadn't fallen in love in her twenties, and by the time she was thirty, she'd ruled out any possibility of marriage.

"I mean it." Paul sounded angry again.

Leah hesitated. Her heart was racing with hope. For the first time in her life she had a chance at real happiness, a promise of something more than she'd ever dared dream. A family. Home. Love. Yes, it had all belonged to her sister, but Diane had come to her in the dream. Diane had sent her to Paul and the children.

"Are you saying you'd be willing to marry me?" she asked in a rush.

Paul buried his hands in his pockets. "Yes. If it wasn't so unfair to you."

"Unfair?"

"Leah, look around you! I'm raising three motherless children. I'll be paying Diane's hospital bills for the next two years and —"

"I know all that."

"I don't have anything to offer you."

Only a wealth beyond her wildest dreams — a wealth that had nothing to do with material things. He was offering her more love than she'd ever thought to find.

"What about the children I love? A home? A family?"

When Paul's gaze connected with hers, he looked uncertain. "That would be enough for you?"

Leah nodded.

His voice was gruff with emotion when he spoke. "Will you marry me, Leah, for all our sakes?"

In a heartbeat. "Yes," she whispered. "Yes, I'll marry you, Paul."

SEVEN

"We're mature adults," Leah said as solemnly as she could. "We both realize this isn't a love match."

"We're going into this with our eyes wide open," Paul agreed.

"Exactly." The relief she felt knowing she wouldn't be forced to leave the children was so great that Leah slumped in the kitchen chair, holding up her head with both hands. She brushed loose strands of hair from her forehead and smiled weakly up at Paul.

"There is love involved, though," Paul said pointedly, studying her.

She'd never been more aware of a man's look. Engrossed in it. Absorbed. Since the night they'd kissed, she'd noticed that the way Paul looked at her had changed. Once again she wished she was more experienced in relationships, because she couldn't say exactly *how* it had changed — or what it meant. He seemed to watch her more closely, his gaze bolder, less veiled. She glanced up to see that he was still waiting for her to respond to his statement.

"Naturally there's love involved," she said, speaking too quickly. "We both love the children," she added, hating the breathless quality of her words.

Paul pulled out a chair and sat across from her. "The children are a vitally important part of this, but there's more involved here. I want to know what you feel for me."

Leah had come to know a directness about Paul that she loved . . . and feared. Her own manner was more subtle and she tended to think more slowly and methodically. To her, every aspect of a problem needed to be analyzed and then logically examined. It was the way she lived her life.

Paul, on the other hand, had neither the time nor the patience to mull over any issue. He wrote to a deadline, and believed that it shouldn't take more than five minutes to think through a situation.

Defining feelings seemed to come more easily to him, as well. Leah had always found that difficult.

"Leah?" Paul prodded when she didn't answer right away.

"I . . . I don't know what I feel for you." It was an honest answer . . . as honest as she dared. She was afraid to love him, and even more afraid that she already did. He made her experience emotions, physical desires, that she hadn't known she was capable of feeling.

"What do you expect from this marriage?" Paul asked her next.

"I don't know that, either. I haven't had time to think about it." Then it struck her, something she should've considered much earlier. "What exactly do *you* expect?"

"A wife."

He left it at that, left it for her to fill in the blanks. "I . . . see."

"Do you, Leah? After we're married, I'll want you to move into my bedroom, share my life and my bed." He hesitated as though he expected an argument. "I realize you don't love me now, but I'm hoping you will in time. Do you have a problem with that?"

Talking so openly had always made Leah uneasy. She lowered her eyes. "No . . . but do you honestly think we can make a marriage work?"

"Of course. Otherwise I'd never agree to it, and neither would you."

"I've been so obtuse," she said, recalling her conversation with his mother. "I can't believe I was so inconsiderate. I really hadn't given any thought to how the children would feel after I moved out."

"I wasn't thinking too clearly myself."

"It's so unlike me."

"I know. Me, too."

"Why did it take your parents so long to say something?" The concerns Elizabeth raised were valid and should have been voiced sooner, in Leah's opinion.

"I asked my dad the same thing," Paul told her. "He said they'd just thought of all this."

"Well, I'm glad they did — for the children's sake."

Paul merely nodded.

Paul glanced nervously at his watch. He only had an hour for lunch and Leah was already five minutes late. He knew something must have detained her, since she was as punctual as she was honest.

Pacing the hallway outside the licensing office in the King County Courthouse, he thought over the changes of the past two days. For the first time in nearly a week, he'd slept soundly. The erotic fantasies centering on Leah that had cost him several nights' sleep had eased. When he went to bed, he closed his eyes, half-fearing she'd stroll into his mind. A vision of her had made nightly appearances since he'd kissed her. She'd smile seductively at him, and then his imagination would take over, tormenting him for hours on end.

But it hadn't happened since Leah had agreed to marry him. Perhaps that was because he knew it was only a matter of time before he made love to her. He'd made sure the night of his parents' visit that Leah understood theirs would be a real marriage.

There'd been a time, not all that distant, when he would've pleaded with God to help him, pleaded with Diane to forgive him and wallowed in guilt for even thinking of making love to his sister-in-law. He felt an acceptance now, an inevitability.

He *needed* Leah. Not for the physical release her body would yield him, although that was part of it. He needed her the way a man needs the substance of life. Air. Water. Food. Just as she was vital to his children, Leah was vital to him. He woke in the morning, and his first thoughts were of her. During the workday he often found himself looking at his watch and calculating how long it would be before he could go home — to her and his children. He wasn't sure when all this had started to happen or even if it was a good thing. All he knew was that it *was* happening.

Did he love Leah?

Paul didn't know. Certainly what he felt for her was unlike his love for Diane. In the months since her death, Paul had become more objective about his marriage to Leah's younger sister. He loved Diane, heart and soul. He'd never experienced deeper grief than when he'd lost her. She was an unselfish woman, and he knew she wouldn't have wanted him and the children to live alone. He genuinely believed Diane would have approved of his marrying Leah. Of Leah raising her kids.

To Paul's way of thinking, if he were to marry a second time, Leah was the perfect choice. For the obvious reasons, yes, but for less obvious ones, too.

In marrying Leah, he'd still be able to hold on to Diane, remain emotionally faithful to her. The two sisters would be forever linked in his mind, his heart. Leah shared his love for Diane, and that alone averted the potential resentments and problems of a second marriage. Leah wouldn't make unreasonable demands in an effort to force Diane out of his life.

Less than a month ago, if anyone — his father or any of his brothers — had suggested he remarry, Paul would've resisted it, regardless of the proposed partner. Even Leah. He hadn't been ready, emotionally or in any other way.

"Paul!" Leah hurried down the courthouse corridor. "I'm so sorry I'm late."

She looked nice, Paul observed. Her hair was held back on either side by silver clips, and she wore a simple linen dress that skimmed her figure.

"I hope I haven't kept you waiting," she said.

"No more than five minutes. Don't worry about it."

"The babysitter was late, and then I couldn't find a parking place and —"

"You're here now and that's all that matters."

She placed her hand over her heart as though to calm its pounding, and Paul ignored the urge to put his arm around her. He found himself looking for excuses to touch her, but so far had managed not to. His fear was that once he did, he wouldn't be able to stop. A touch would lead to a kiss and a kiss would lead . . . who knew where.

"We apply for the marriage license over here," he said, directing her through a pair of doors.

She nodded, then paused before entering the office. "You're sure you want to go through with this?" she whispered without looking at him.

If either of them was going to entertain second thoughts, the time was now. Yet Paul didn't hesitate. He knew what he wanted; he wanted Leah. "Positive. What about you?"

Her smile was sweet. "I'm here, aren't I?"

Applying for the marriage license took barely five minutes. Paul was glad that Leah had left the kids with a sitter. For the first time since she'd moved in with him, he had uninterrupted time alone with her — away from the house.

"How about lunch?"

His invitation seemed to surprise — and please — her. "I'd like that."

There was a popular bookstore off First Avenue with a small restaurant in the basement. Paul ate there often and enjoyed the feel of the place. It wasn't fancy, or even close to fancy, and it certainly wasn't where a man would take a woman he wanted to impress. But it was a restaurant Paul knew Leah would love.

They stood in line to order, then found a table at the back, next to an old brick wall hung with bookshelves and pieces by local artists.

"This is perfect," Leah said, glancing eagerly around.

"I thought you'd like it."

She smiled shyly. "I have some exciting news."

"Oh?"

"Kelsey took her first step this morning!"

Leah looked as proud as if his daughter had flown to the moon and back on her own power.

"I've been expecting it any day," he said, smiling back at her.

"The boys were as excited as I was."

"I remember when Ryan and Ronnie were that age."

A waitress delivered their chicken pot pies and hot coffee.

Leah reached for her fork. "Who walked first, Ryan or Ronnie?"

"Ryan. He wanted his blankie, and since I was holding it out to him, the most expedient way to collect it was to take a few steps in my direction. As I recall, Ronnie refused to allow his brother to outdo him and walked almost immediately afterward."

"It's hard to remember the boys at a year old," Leah said with a happy sigh.

Paul nodded, then said, "Leah, let's not talk about the children."

Her gaze shot up, and her eyes, which were a vibrant green today, reflecting her pale green dress, revealed her bewilderment.

"Why not?"

"Because we're going to be married soon."

"You . . . want to discuss that?" She sounded worried.

"No. But at some point in the future the children will be gone and there'll be only the two of us. We both love the children. That's a given. We've agreed to get married for our own individual reasons, but in the end it'll come down to the two of us. We need to build a relationship."

"A relationship," she repeated, as though the words felt awkward on her tongue.

"If you prefer, we could call it a friendship."

Leah nodded. "You're right, of course. . . . It's just that I'm not very good at this sort of thing. You'll probably need to help me."

Her confession touched him. After all that Leah had done for him and the children, it gladdened his heart that he could assist her in some small way. He'd make this as easy on her as he could, guide her whenever possible, encourage her to feel confident in her own emotions. If he'd been forced to identify any fault of Leah's, it would be her stubborn self-reliance. He recognized it because he was fiercely independent himself. As the oldest of five children, he'd learned early in life that he had to be.

"What shall we talk about?" Leah asked softly.

"Anything we like."

An earsplitting silence followed. They'd lived together for nearly two months. They'd agreed to marry. They planned to spend the rest of their lives together. Yet when Paul took the children out of the conversation, they had nothing to say.

"Oh, dear," Leah said, her eyes filled with alarm. She set down her fork. "This is more difficult than I realized."

"Do you want to tell me about your garden, Mary, Mary, Quite Contrary?"

Her eyes brightened, but after a moment the enthusiasm drained away. "What's there to tell you? It's growing nicely."

"My parents keep a garden," Paul volunteered.

"Do they grow herbs?"

"Not to my knowledge."

"What about zucchini?"

"Enough to feed the entire state," Paul said. His dad routinely dropped off huge quantities of the vegetable. Paul hadn't the heart to tell him he'd rather eat gravel than zucchini. At least Diane had found a recipe — zucchini chocolate cake — that made it tolerable.

Their conversation got off to a slow start,

but by the end of the hour, Paul felt they'd made some real headway.

When they'd finished their lunch, Paul walked Leah back to where she'd parked the car. Although he was late getting back to the office, he found himself reluctant to leave. He'd be home in a matter of hours, but he wanted to hold on to this time alone with her.

Leah didn't seem eager to leave, either. She held her car keys in one hand, glancing down at them periodically.

Suddenly he felt an impulse to kiss her. But it wasn't the kind of thing he was comfortable doing on a busy Seattle street. He knew any public display of affection would only embarrass Leah. Diane would've spontaneously thrown her arms around his neck and kissed him regardless of where they were or who was watching.

But it wasn't Diane he was marrying; it was Leah.

Leah woke on the morning of her wedding day to bright sunshine. Paul had contacted a minister acquaintance who'd agreed to perform a private ceremony at his office, with the minister's wife and his youth pastor serving as witnesses.

They'd arranged everything quickly, quietly. They hadn't said anything to Paul's family. Leah wasn't sure Paul intended to say anything until afterward, which suited her fine. Being hovered over by his mother would've made Leah more nervous than she already was.

She didn't doubt that she was doing the right thing in marrying Paul, but she preferred to do it without formalities. His family would've insisted on making a production out of it, which wasn't at all what Leah wanted.

She'd purchased a white linen suit for the ceremony. Normally she didn't wear a hat, but she'd found one she rather liked. The salesclerk had been very helpful, and Leah was grateful for the extra touch of style.

Diane had always gone with her when she needed to buy something for a special occasion. How ironic that Leah had never craved her sister's opinion more than she had while trying to choose what to wear when she married Paul.

The ceremony itself took only minutes. Filling out the marriage license had been more complicated than the wedding itself. They'd decided on plain gold bands and Paul's eyes, warm and reassuring, had held hers when he'd slipped the ring on her finger.

It had seemed appropriate to have the children with them; Kelsey stood between the two boys who held her hands, and all three stared wide-eyed as their father married Leah.

Afterward Paul kissed her briefly. Although his mouth had barely grazed hers, a riot of sensations came rushing at Leah. She trembled in his arms and prayed he hadn't guessed how strong her response had been.

When they left the church office, Paul suggested they visit his parents. Leah agreed. The children would need their afternoon naps soon, but there was time for a short visit.

Elizabeth looked mildly surprised when she opened her front door. "Paul, Leah," she greeted them cheerfully, holding the screen door. "Come in, please." She took Kelsey from Paul's arms and set her on the carpet. "I hear she's walking now."

"Just watch. This kid's headed for the Olympics at the rate she's going," Paul said, smiling.

"Paul." His father strolled into the living room, looking delighted by their unexpected arrival. "Sit down, sit down."

Leah sat on the couch and Paul joined her. The boys hurried to the kitchen and stood by the counter, waiting for their grandmother to offer them the cookie jar.

Elizabeth complied with a smile, then walked into the living room. If Paul's parents noticed that he and Leah were overdressed for an early Saturday afternoon, neither commented.

Paul reached for Leah's hand, squeezed her fingers with his own, then looked at his parents. "Leah and I stopped by to tell you we've taken your advice. We were married about an hour ago."

"Married!" his mother cried.

"Married!" his father boomed, vaulting to his feet.

Perplexed, Leah turned to look at her husband. Perhaps they'd misunderstood. Perhaps that *wasn't* what his parents had meant. But Leah had been so sure. . . .

Elizabeth started to weep softly.

"Mom?" Paul made no effort to disguise his confusion. "Good grief, I'd think you'd be happy."

"I am."

"Then why the tears?"

"Because you're just like Taylor and Christy."

"Don't forget Rich," Eric snapped.

"What do the girls have to do with Leah and me?"

"First, Taylor married Russ in Reno. She

163

didn't have a single family member there. Not one. Your father and I could've flown there in less than two hours. Out of the blue she marries a cowboy she's known less than three months."

"Then Christy married Cody," Eric went on. "In Idaho, no less. She flies to a neighboring state to get married for fear her family might find out about it."

"If you'll recall," Paul added wryly, "she was still engaged to James at the time. She felt she had no other choice."

"She didn't even let Taylor in on what she was doing, not until much later." Elizabeth wiped the tears from her face. "If it wasn't bad enough that your sisters married without family present, Rich had an ordinary judge marry him and Jamie."

"That's because they were planning their divorce shortly afterward," Paul said, defending his brother. "Besides, we were married by a minister, not a judge, if that's any consolation."

"Wait. He was planning a divorce?" Confused, Leah whispered the question in Paul's ear.

"I'll tell you later," he promised.

Vaguely Leah remembered Diane describing the details of Rich's marriage to Jamie Warren. As she recalled, the couple had originally gotten married for the purpose of having a child. Diane had explained that they'd planned for Jamie to be artificially inseminated, but when she did become pregnant, there hadn't been anything artificial about it.

"You're upset because we didn't invite you to the ceremony?" Paul asked his parents, who shared an incredulous look.

"Yes." His father's loud voice echoed through the house. "What is it with you kids? Don't you have any idea how badly your mother and I want to attend a wedding in this family? We have five children, four of them now married, and we've yet to be invited to a single child's wedding."

"Dad, Mom, I'm sorry," Paul said, sounding genuinely contrite.

Leah felt terrible. She should've encouraged Paul to mention their decision to his family. She hadn't done so for selfish reasons. She was afraid Elizabeth would make a fuss, something Leah had wanted to avoid.

"I apologize, too," Leah said meekly.

"It's done now," Eric said, tight-lipped. Then he made an effort to relax. "But you're making a habit of this, son," he muttered, referring to Paul's first wedding in Alaska.

"I promise if I ever get married again, I'll

165

make sure you and Mom are there for it."

Although she knew Paul was joking, Leah felt a small twinge of anxiety and possessiveness.

"Jason's our last hope for a family wedding," Elizabeth said, dabbing her eyes with a tissue she'd taken from her pocket.

"Jason," Paul repeated, barely holding back a laugh. "I hate to disappoint you, but I can't see Jason ever getting married. He's too set in his ways."

"God's going to find that son of mine a wife," Elizabeth said. "I can't believe the good Lord would give me five beautiful children and then cheat me out of the pleasure of putting on even one wedding."

"I'm sure everything will work out for the best," Paul said in a soothing voice.

The boys started squabbling, and Leah knew it was because they were tired and hadn't had their lunch. Kelsey was about to fall asleep, as well.

"We should be going," Leah said, turning to Paul. "I feel really bad that we disappointed you," she added to the Mannings. "I hope you'll forgive us for being so thoughtless." She stood, reaching for Kelsey. The little girl laid her head against Leah's shoulder and yawned sleepily.

"Where are you two going for your honeymoon?" Eric asked.

Paul and Leah exchanged shocked glances. "We hadn't planned a honeymoon," Paul replied.

"I certainly hope you intend to get away for the night, at least."

Paul frowned apologetically at Leah. "Actually I . . . we hadn't discussed it."

"That's no excuse," Elizabeth said immediately. "Leave the children with your father and me, and the two of you take the rest of the day and tonight for yourselves."

Leah wanted to object, but was immediately cut off. "But —"

"There's no but about it. You're family now, although I've always considered you part of our family anyway. Now it's official. And I won't allow this cantankerous son of mine to deprive his bride of a honeymoon."

"What about the children's things?"

"You can bring them over later. I'll give them lunch and put them down for a nap and everything will be just fine, won't it, boys?"

Spending time with their grandparents had always been a special treat, and the twins were eager for the opportunity.

"You're positive this isn't too much trouble?" Leah murmured. Since Kelsey was already asleep, Leah carried her to the crib set up in the Mannings' spare bedroom.

"No problem whatsoever," Elizabeth insisted. "You and Paul go and have a nice uninterrupted day. I'll drop the children off after church in the morning."

"This is so nice of you."

"Nonsense." Paul's mother hugged her. "I'm so happy for you and Paul. I couldn't imagine him finding a better wife."

Leah had no illusions about her marriage. As she and Paul had discussed earlier, theirs wasn't a love match — although Paul had made sure she understood she'd be sharing his bed. But for all intents and purposes, it was a marriage of convenience.

Convenient for him. Convenient for the children. Convenient for her.

"Thank you again," Leah said when Paul's mother escorted her to the front door.

Paul helped her into the car. The twins and their grandparents stood on the front lawn and waved as he started the car and they drove away.

Paul was quiet for several minutes, and without the children as a buffer, Leah felt awkward and ill at ease.

"I'm sorry, Leah," he finally said.

"For what?"

"For cheating you."

"Cheating me? I don't understand." She

didn't feel the least bit slighted. Her wedding was exactly the way she'd wanted it. Intimate, with only the children present.

"Mom and Dad were right. I should've planned a honeymoon trip for us. It was inconsiderate of me."

"I don't want a trip."

"Perhaps not, but you deserve one. You deserve a whole lot more than I'm giving you." He sounded angry, but his disappointment was obviously directed at himself and not at her.

"Stop right this minute, Paul Manning."

"Stop? We're on the freeway."

She sighed. "I was speaking figuratively."

"Oh."

"It's not your job to read my mind. If I want something, I'll ask for it. All right?"

"All right."

A few minutes passed. "What about our wedding night?"

"What about it?" Leah felt uneasy discussing the subject.

"Do you want to go to a hotel?"

"No." Her response was immediate. A hotel would only make her more nervous than she was already.

"Why not?"

"Well . . . because . . . you might feel pressured to make love to me."

"Feel pressured?" She thought she detected a note of humor in his tone.

"I . . . I think our marriage would be better served if we delayed the . . . physical aspect of our relationship, don't you? I mean . . . what I'm trying to say is that, well, we hardly have anything to talk about without the children. Remember what it was like at lunch the other day? It makes sense to me that we should develop a solid friendship before we . . . you know."

"The term is make love," Paul returned impatiently.

"Right . . . before we make love." It was difficult for her to speak so openly, but she made the effort because too much was at stake. They had their whole lives before them. It seemed to her there was plenty of time to become comfortable with each other before beginning the sexual part of their marriage.

"You agree, don't you?" she asked timidly.

Paul didn't answer right away. "We'll sleep in the same bed."

He left no room for doubt. "If you want," she said.

"I certainly do."

"I'm agreeable to that." Leah found herself wishing they'd discussed this earlier.

"What about tonight?" he demanded. "If

you don't want to go to a hotel, how do you suggest we spend the night?"

Leah hesitated. "Would you mind if we just stayed home?"

EIGHT

"You want to stay home." Paul was sure he hadn't heard her right. Not only had she chosen to skip a honeymoon, but she also wanted to ignore their wedding night. If it was what she really wanted, then fine, he could accept that. He didn't like it, but he could accept it. But staying home, that was another matter entirely.

"There's so much to do," she was saying.

"Like what?"

"I . . . thought I'd use this afternoon to move my stuff into your bedroom."

"Good idea. But what about tonight?"

"Tonight?" she echoed, her voice slightly raised with what sounded like nervousness.

"We should do something special."

"I thought . . . we already decided . . . not to, you know . . . haven't we? We'd agreed to hold off on the —"

"I was thinking more along the lines of going out to dinner."

"Oh."

The silence between them was filled with tension.

"Don't worry, Leah, I'm not going to ravish you." Paul didn't know how this marriage was going to survive with Leah's current attitude. He'd only kissed her twice. The first time had been one of the most sensual experiences of his life. The second had been at the end of their wedding ceremony, and although it had been little more than a brushing of lips, Paul had felt a hot current of need surge between them. She could deny it if she chose, but he wasn't going to.

Yet, despite the intensity of their attraction, Leah seemed determined to follow through with this self-imposed abstinence. Paul didn't really understand why, and it frustrated him.

When his parents had offered to take the children, Paul had entertained thoughts of bringing Leah home, carrying her over the threshold and directly into his bedroom. He'd envisioned an afternoon of introducing her to the physical delights of marriage. After dinner, he'd introduce her all over again.

He pulled into the driveway, turned off the engine and sat for a few minutes, trying to collect his thoughts.

"We can go out to dinner, if you like," she said weakly.

He nodded. Starting their marriage with an argument wasn't a healthy sign, especially since they'd never spoken crossly to each other before. Apparently they'd been saving all their arguing for the so-called honeymoon.

Paul went around to open her car door, and Leah smiled tremulously up at him. Try as he might, he couldn't resist her and returned the smile.

So she wanted to build a solid relationship before they made love. He supposed he could understand that. He himself tended to see physical love as part of developing a relationship, but he realized she didn't. For her, that came later, after common ground had been established between them.

Okay, he could live with it.

He prayed he could live with it.

Once inside the house, they moved into their separate bedrooms and changed clothes. As Paul loosened his tie, he wondered just how long Leah felt they should hold off. He walked over to the closet and stood there, staring blankly at the row of clothes.

Would she make him wait a week? He

could endure a week.

What about a month? Nope. Out of the question.

He removed his shirt, then, sitting on the end of the bed, he untied one shoe and slipped it off his foot.

He didn't realize he'd been there so long, mulling over the situation, until he heard Leah outside the bedroom.

"Paul?"

"Yes."

"I'm ready to bring in some of my things."

"Just a minute." He finished changing in record time, then opened the door. She stood there in a loose shirt and faded jeans, holding a load of clothes in her arms. Paul took them from her and carried them to the bed.

"I was thinking I could move my things, and you could take the children's stuff over to your parents'."

"Sure," he said amicably enough. He wasn't eager to leave her, but it might be for the best. He'd put the time to good use, ponder what he was going to do about this nonmarriage-marriage.

"Do you want some lunch before you go? You must be starved — you didn't have anything to eat this morning, did you? I know I didn't."

"No, thanks." He shoved his car keys into his jeans pocket.

"But aren't you hungry?"

His eyes found hers. "Yes, Leah, I'm hungry," he informed her. "I'm starving to death."

His exit made for excellent drama, but it didn't do anything to improve his mood.

They were married. He had the legal document to prove it. And yet he couldn't enjoy the rights and privileges of marriage. . . .

Paul hadn't come to any conclusions by the time he returned to the house. His poor parents must be wondering what was going on. He'd parked in their driveway, gotten out of the car, walked to the door, waited until his mother answered, handed her the clothes Leah had packed for the kids and a fresh stack of diapers for Kelsey, turned around and left.

He thought he might've heard his mother call after him, but if that was the case, he'd ignored her. He also thought he might've heard his father chuckling, telling Paul's mother she should recognize a man in a hurry when she saw one.

Paul was in a hurry, all right, but he didn't have anywhere to go.

Back at the house, Leah had emptied her

bedroom and transported her clothes, books and assorted paraphernalia into his. A lot of good sleeping in the same bed was going to do them.

"I . . . fixed you some lunch."

"Thanks." He made the effort to smile as he walked into the kitchen.

She followed but stayed several feet behind. What did she think, he was going to attack her?

"You're angry with me, aren't you?" she asked, folding her hands.

"No."

"You are. I can tell. . . . I told you I'm not good at these things. Di— My sister was always so much better at dealing with emotions . . . Dealing with men, too. You regret marrying me already and . . ."

She sounded close to tears. Whatever anger or frustration Paul was experiencing died a sudden death. He walked over to her and took her in his arms, wanting to ease her distress.

"I'm sorry," he breathed into her hair, loving the feel of her in his arms. With his finger he brushed a strand of hair from her face.

"I feel like a total failure as a wife and we haven't even been married a day. I'm sorry. . . ." He heard the tears in her voice and he felt like the biggest jerk who'd ever lived. He'd behaved like a little boy who'd had his candy taken away from him. If anyone was to blame, he was the one.

"No, *I'm* sorry," he whispered.

"You?" She lifted her head and looked up at him. "Why?"

"Because I've acted like a major jerk."

"You're disappointed because I wanted to wait before we . . . made love?"

He nodded.

"I . . . I didn't think you'd want me. Not really."

"Not want you?"

She lowered her eyes and went completely still. The only movement was the rise and fall of her chest as she breathed. "I'm not very pretty."

"Leah, for heaven's sake, you're so beautiful you take my breath away!"

"Please don't lie to me. I know my assets and my weaknesses and —"

Paul reacted instinctively, framing her face in his hands, his eyes on hers. Whatever else she'd intended to say disappeared as his mouth claimed hers. He'd obviously caught her off guard. Leah braced her hands against his chest and, after a moment of surprise, parted her lips to him.

Paul groaned. He hurt. He ached. He

wanted her so badly. . . .

Leah groaned, too, and he took her mouth again, this time long and slow instead of hungry and demanding. Paul found himself drowning in hot sensation. He had to touch her. . . .

Leah groaned anew.

"Am I hurting you?"

"No."

"Frightening you?"

"Yes."

He started to move away.

"No," she pleaded, clutching his wrist. "What frightens me are the wonderful things you make me feel."

Paul kissed her again. And again. He kissed her softly. Then quickly. Teasingly. Slowly.

Leah's eyes fluttered open with disappointment when he stopped. They were brown-green now and hazy with passion. "Paul?"

"Hmm . . ."

"I . . ."

"You're beautiful."

She stiffened, but Paul continued to hold her. "I love the color of your eyes. They intrigue me, the way they change. So many shades of color, of meaning . . ."

She blushed, but Paul hadn't even begun

to tell her everything he found exquisite about her. "You have no idea how beautiful your hair looks in the sunlight." He wanted to tell her about the afternoon he'd watched her working in the backyard with the children around her, but he couldn't find the words.

"I love your mouth."

He kissed her to prove it.

"Paul." She sighed.

"But most of all," he said, "I love your laugh."

"Oh, Paul."

"So don't you dare tell me you're not beautiful."

"You make me want to cry."

Paul smiled. "You've helped dry *my* tears, Leah." He paused. "I want you so much."

"You do?"

"Are you sure you want to wait?" Paul whispered.

"Uh . . . I'm not sure of anything at the moment."

His fingers were busy unfastening the buttons of her shirt. "What about this?" he asked. "Maybe . . ."

How or when they made it from the kitchen to the bedroom, Paul didn't know.

They collapsed onto his bed together. As they cuddled there, kissing, she suddenly began to squirm. "We can't," she said breathlessly.

"Why not?"

"Because . . . because there's someone . . . here."

Only then did Paul hear the persistent peal of the doorbell. "What the hell," he said, bolting off the bed. He didn't bother to put on his shirt as he marched out of the bedroom and to the front door.

He jerked it open to see Jason — baseball cap on his head and bat in his hand.

"What do you want?" Paul snarled.

"Paul," Leah said from somewhere behind him, her voice the cool mist of reason.

"It's Jason," he said, turning around to face her.

"Don't you think you should invite him in?"

"Frankly, no."

Jason, however, didn't wait for an invitation and strolled boldly into the house. He paused in the middle of the living room and seemed to notice Paul's disheveled state for the first time. Leah was quickly buttoning her shirt, gazing up at his brother with reddened cheeks, clearly wondering why she'd ever left the bedroom.

"I don't suppose I've dropped in at an inauspicious time, have I?" Jason asked, grinning from ear to ear.

Leah had never been more embarrassed in her life. Her face felt fiery hot.

Jason didn't seem at all disturbed. Paul looked just plain angry.

Both men, however, were staring at her as if *she* should be the one to explain. "We're married," she said after an awkward moment.

"Married." Jason's already broad smile widened. "When did this happen?"

Paul looked at the living room clock. "Three and a half hours ago. You just interrupted my wedding night, so to speak. This better be good."

"Anyone else know?" Jason leaned indolently on his baseball bat, crossing his ankles.

"Mom and Dad."

"They've got the children," Leah said as she turned away. Her shirt was misbuttoned. She hurried to the master bedroom and searched for her bra. By the time she returned, properly dressed, she'd managed to compose herself somewhat.

Jason had plopped himself down on the couch, resting his ankle on his knee. He was completely at ease, arms stretched out on either side.

"So you're married."

"You want to see the proof?" Paul asked.

Jason's gaze meandered over to Leah. "I already have."

Paul's arms circled her waist, bringing her close. "I take it this unexpected visit has a purpose."

"Yeah. But I'm having so much fun watching Leah blush, I thought I'd delay getting around to it a bit longer."

"If you value your neck, little brother, you'll get to the point right now."

Jason rubbed the side of his jaw. "As I recall, Rich interrupted Christy and Cody's wedding night, too. Must be a family habit."

"Jason!"

Paul's brother chuckled and uncrossed his legs. "Actually, it's a bit of a bad-news/good-news story."

"Give me the bad news first."

"John Duncan, the shortstop you replaced, was hurt this afternoon."

"Playing ball?" Leah hadn't realized softball was so dangerous.

"No," Jason assured her. "He tripped over something in the parking lot and sprained his ankle. Looks like he'll be out for the rest of the season."

"What's the good news?" Paul asked suspiciously.

"The team has elected you as a permanent replacement."

Leah's heart swelled with pleasure. Paul loved softball. The two weeks he'd played on his brother's team had done him so much good. He'd come home enthusiastic and happy. She couldn't understand his hesitation now.

"What's the matter?" Jason asked. "I thought you'd be pleased."

"I'm a family man."

"So?" Jason argued. "Rich has got a family, too, and he plays."

Slowly, his face devoid of expression, Paul turned to Leah. "What do you think?"

She nodded eagerly. "I think it'd be wonderful."

"You won't mind?"

"Of course not!"

"Then it's settled," Jason said, springing effortlessly to his feet. "I'll go now and let the two of you get back to your . . . honeymoon." He paused when he reached the front door. "This isn't supposed to be a secret, is it?"

"No." It was Paul who answered.

"Good. Then it's okay if I tell a few choice folks — like your brother, for instance. Rich? Remember him? And his wife?"

A smile appeared on Paul's face. "It's fine

with me." He glanced at her. "Leah?"

She nodded.

"Great. See you two lovebirds later."

Lovebirds. The word leapt out at Leah. If Jason hadn't arrived when he did, she and Paul would've made love. Despite all the very good reasons she'd assembled in her mind. Despite the fact that they weren't in love. Despite the fact that she wasn't emotionally ready to deal with the complexities of a sexual relationship. Despite all that, they would have made love.

Leah walked into the kitchen and stood by the sink, staring out at the backyard.

Paul followed her.

"I know what you're thinking," he said, standing behind her.

Leah doubted it. "What?"

"You'd still prefer if we waited before we make love."

"Yes!" She whirled around to face him. "How'd you know that?"

His smile drooped. "Because I'd prefer to wait, too."

Paul changed his mind fifteen times in the next fifteen minutes, and a hundred more times as the evening progressed. Jason calling them *lovebirds* was what convinced him Leah had been right about holding off on the lovemaking.

The word had the same effect on him as a punch to the stomach. Did he *love* Leah? Paul didn't know. He was physically hungry for her. He admired and trusted her. He was grateful to her. He appreciated her. He found her generous and sweet.

But did he love her?

That was the one question Paul couldn't answer. He loved Diane. He could never stop loving her. But if he loved Diane, was it possible to love Leah at the same time?

This was another question for which Paul didn't have an answer.

Although he'd rationalized marriage and a physical relationship between them — Diane wouldn't have wanted him to be alone — he discovered the justification no longer eased his mind. He had no way of really knowing what Diane would've wanted.

Diane had been his wife. But now he was married to Leah. Where did that leave him?

Married to one.

Devoted to the other.

That was where it left him. Exactly where he'd been weeks earlier. One foot in the present, the other in the past. Torn between two sisters.

One alive.

The other dead.

Married to both.

Paul took Leah out to dinner that night. A fancy restaurant. Expensive, elegant. He'd already robbed her of so many of the things a wife was entitled to. A courtship, for one.

Leah was a beautiful, generous woman, but she'd been the only one giving in their relationship. It angered Paul that he'd been so oblivious to her needs.

Not only had Leah been deprived of a courtship, but she hadn't even had a decent wedding — a ceremony with flowers and music, family and friends. Instead he'd rushed her to a preacher friend, not even the minister at the church they attended. He'd married her before strangers, as though he was ashamed.

As the evening went on, Paul felt even worse. He'd cheated this warm, gracious woman out of so much. He wondered how long it would take him to make it up to her. He knew one thing. He'd do it before he made any physical demands on her.

Leah deserved that much.

Leah wasn't sure what she should expect of married life with Paul. After the first week, she was more confused than ever. Other than that first afternoon, Paul had hardly touched her. He kissed her cheek before he left for the office and again when he came home. But that was the extent of their physical contact.

Yet he'd never been more generous. He frequently brought her small gifts. A red rose on Monday. Bubble bath on Wednesday. A huge chocolate-chip cookie on Friday.

Leah didn't know what to make of the changes in him. He was patient and gentle. Tender in ways she hadn't expected. He praised her efforts, complimented her on her meals and on how clean the house was or how happy the children seemed. He complimented her, too, on her appearance — her hair, the clothes she wore, her eyes.

This was all well and good. But Leah longed to be a wife. A real wife. Not just a stand-in wife and mother, a replacement for her sister.

And she wanted all this even though she'd told him she'd prefer to wait. . . . She was embarrassed by her contradictory response to him. Yes, she felt that a sexual relationship shouldn't take place until they knew each other well. And yet . . . And yet . . .

Nights were the worst for Leah. After dinner Paul generally worked on his novel. He did this once the children were in bed — he always helped her with the twins and with Kelsey. But as soon as they were down for the evening, he retreated to his den.

Although he'd never said as much, not that he ever would, Leah was convinced his sudden focus on the novel was a convenient way to avoid being alone with her.

It might not have hurt so much if he hadn't kissed her and loved her so sweetly the first afternoon they were married. If he *hadn't* kissed her and told her how beautiful she was to him, she might never have known what she was missing.

But she did know.

She couldn't tell him, though; she just couldn't. And she certainly couldn't *ask* him to make love to her. Maybe some women could, but not Leah.

They slept in the same bed, but they might as well be in different countries for all the space Paul maintained between them.

All three of the children could have slept comfortably between them. And sometimes they did.

Ryan and Ronnie were pleased that their aunt Leah was now their daddy's wife. Leah wasn't convinced they understood the implications, except that she'd moved into the bedroom with their dad and they could have their playroom back.

Nearly two weeks after their wedding, Leah was absolutely sure Paul never intended to make love to her. She was busy arranging a vase of cut flowers after dinner on Friday evening when he came into the kitchen. The kids were asleep, and the night was gently warm.

Paul poured himself a cup of coffee.

"How's the writing?" she asked, keeping up the facade.

"Slow."

"Do you want to talk about the scene?" They did that sometimes.

"No."

His refusal hurt a little. If he hadn't been so loving toward her in so many other ways, Leah would've felt even worse. She gave him a smile of encouragement and returned to her task.

A half hour later she was leaving the bathroom — her hair damp, wearing a cool cotton gown — just as Paul came into the hallway. He stopped when he saw her. His blue eyes looked wild.

Neither moved.

Leah could see every breath he took. She watched the pulse hammering in his neck and felt the tension that seemed to throb through his body.

Right then Leah sensed that he wanted

her. It wasn't tension she saw in him but desire.

"Paul," she whispered, holding out her hand. "I . . . I want to be your wife." Her voice was shaky; she couldn't help that. This was as close as she could come to asking. His reaction to her was an invitation; she knew that. An invitation she was going to accept.

He closed his eyes. "You're . . . ready?"

She nodded. "I'm ready."

"There'll be no turning back."

"I know."

He took one step toward her and she met him halfway. He wrapped his arms around her waist and lifted her from the floor until her mouth was level with his own. Then he kissed her with an urgency that stole the breath from her lungs.

NINE

Leah had finally, finally given him the signal he'd been waiting for. Hoping for.

In the past two weeks Paul had tried to court her, show her how grateful he was to have her in his life. He'd brought her small gifts. But they seemed insignificant and couldn't begin to express everything that was in his heart. If anything, the gifts seemed to embarrass her more than they pleased her.

He wanted to talk openly with her, explain what was on his mind, but found it impossible. To his credit, during the first week of courting her, his motives had been pure. It was torture sleeping with Leah beside him without touching her. No small feat, he realized, particularly now that he held her in his arms.

The second week, his vision of what he'd hoped to accomplish had blurred, his original objective obscured by his growing frustration. Soon he'd lost track of just about everything, except what he was denying himself. At night he closeted himself in his home office, because being alone with her and not touching her was just too difficult.

Now that she was voluntarily in his arms, Paul wanted no room for misunderstanding. This time, what they started, they would finish. Like he'd told her, there was no turning back.

His hands were eager as he carefully pulled off her cotton nightgown. She must have sensed his excited perusal. Her gaze skirted shyly past him as she smiled. Paul reached out and placed his hand against the side of her face. She pressed her own hand over his.

"Second thoughts?"

Her gaze dropped as she shook her head. "None."

"Good." Which had to be the understatement of the century.

All that was left between them was the richness of their desire. All that was left was a beauty that overwhelmed him. A radiance that transcended them both.

"Oh, Paul," she whispered afterward, her eyes bright with tears. "I never realized it could be so beautiful." She combed her fingers through his hair and brought his mouth back to hers. "I didn't think you'd ever want to make love to me."

"Me not make . . . not want . . . never . . ." The words twisted themselves around the end of his tongue. "I've been doing everything but cartwheels in the garden trying to get you to notice me. What do you need, woman, smoke signals?"

Leah chuckled softly. "I doubt it would've done any good."

"Why not?"

"Because I've discovered that, for all your brilliance, you can be pretty dense."

"Who, me?"

"If anyone needed to send smoke signals, it was me."

Paul was floored. "Are you trying to tell me you —"

She nodded. "I wanted to say something . . . but I couldn't. I didn't know how. Anyway, you kept avoiding me."

"Avoiding you?" He couldn't believe his ears. "I had to escape because I didn't trust myself alone with you. Leah, I've been crazy for you since before we got married."

"You have?"

It shocked him that she was genuinely surprised to hear it. "You've kept me waiting nearly two weeks."

"I'm . . . not very good at letting you know my feelings, am I?"

He smiled down at her. "Remember, I'm not a mind reader. You're going to have to tell me what you want."

She nodded — and kissed him again.

At work Paul's mind wandered. There was probably a word for what was happening between him and Leah; he just didn't know what it was. Not long ago, they'd only communicated about the children or the household or occasionally his book. Now they were profoundly, intimately, attuned to each other.

Simply put, he *needed* Leah. He felt a sense of freedom in making love to her. Freedom and joy. A joy so great it all but sang from his heart. He expected to feel remorse and guilt, and had been almost giddy with relief when he felt neither. The first night he'd made love to her he'd lain awake and waited for the guilt to come crashing in on him. It hadn't.

He wasn't certain exactly what he *should* be feeling. If not guilt, then what?

He had loved Diane. He loved her still. That confused him even more. If he cared so deeply for Diane, then how was it possible to love Leah as much as he did?

For the first time in months, Paul was feeling something other than emotional pain, and it felt good. He didn't want to do anything that might threaten the happiness Leah had brought him.

Just thinking about his wife, at home waiting for him, made Paul rush out of the office. He found he did that most evenings now, eager to get home to his family. He'd hug his children and then bide his time until he could be with his wife, with Leah, alone.

Tonight he could hardly wait for the kids to go to bed after dinner. When they protested, saying it was still light outside, Paul appeased the twins by reading them a story. He tucked them in and within minutes they were asleep.

Then he walked into the kitchen, where Leah was cleaning up after bathing Kelsey and putting her to bed. She glanced over at him and smiled shyly.

There was a sweet innocence about her that got to him. He'd look at her a certain way, and she'd blush. He'd discovered that he loved to make her blush. She was very different in that regard from Diane and it entranced him.

"Leah." He moved up behind her and slipped his arms around her waist. He nuzzled her neck. "Let's go to bed," he whispered.

She turned slightly. "Paul, I think we should talk."

"Later," he promised, kissing the side of her face. "We'll do all the talking you want later. I promise."

"The boys . . . they just went down."

"They're asleep. I made sure of that."

"But . . ."

He was surprised by her resistance. Not once since that first night had she offered even a token protest.

"All right," he said, dragging in a deep breath. "What's wrong?"

"I . . . don't know."

"Obviously something's bothering you."

"Yes . . ." She stayed where she was, her back to him. "What about Diane?" she said in a low voice.

"What about her?"

"Do you . . . do you pretend —"

"No." He didn't allow her to finish because he knew what she was going to ask. "Not once have I made love to you and thought of her. Not once." He said it emphatically, so there'd be no doubt in her mind.

"Then . . . then what *do* you think about?"

He said the first thing that came to him.

The truth. "How much I want you, how much you satisfy me. How grateful I am that you're in my life — and in my bed."

She turned to face him and slowly raised her eyes to his, studying his expression, seeking some outward sign that he was telling her the truth.

He reached for her hand and brought it to his lips. "It's true, Leah."

He kissed her then, astonished by the sweetness and the power of her kiss.

"You're *sure* the boys are asleep?" she asked in a whisper-thin voice. "I know Kelsey is . . ."

"Yes," Paul said, urging her toward the bedroom.

She didn't hesitate.

When they lay in each other's arms, satisfied and exhausted, Paul returned to the worry she'd confided in him a little earlier.

"Please believe me when I say I've never, ever, confused you with Diane. I need you, Leah. Not because of the way we make love together, and not because of all the help you've given me with the children. I don't know exactly when it happened or even why, but I need you in my life. To laugh with me. To share the joy of raising my children, to share the grief of losing someone we both deeply loved."

Paul's hands abandoned hers and moved to softly caress her face. "I call myself a writer, work with words every day, yet I can't find the words I need now. I wish I could say everything I feel for you. I wish I could explain what's in my heart. . . ."

His mouth took her, and, sighing, she lifted her arms and slid them around his neck.

The phone on the bedside table rang just then, and Paul groaned and broke away. He let it ring a second time and a third as he tried to compose himself before answering.

"Hello." Despite his effort he knew he sounded gruff and impatient.

"Paul, it's Rich. Got a minute?"

Paul's eyes met Leah's and he grinned. That was about as long as he was willing to spare. "Yeah, a minute."

"Jamie and I were talking. Actually, Jason was in on the discussion, too."

"What discussion?"

"I'm getting around to that, so quit being so impatient. We all want to take you and Leah out to dinner Saturday night. Sort of a welcome-to-the-family thing for Leah. We should've done it sooner, but with Mom and Dad out of town . . . Anyway, better late than never."

It took an instant for his brother's words to sink in. He turned his face away from his wife because looking at Leah was too distracting.

"What did you say?" he muttered. "Dinner?"

"Yeah, dinner. Saturday night for you and Leah. Uh, do you want me to call back later?"

"No, that's okay. We'll need to find a sitter, but that shouldn't be too difficult."

"Mom and Dad will want to hold a reception for the two of you when they're back from Montana, but that's not going to be for a month."

"Or more."

"Exactly," Rich said. "It's too long to wait. We all like Leah and want to make sure she feels welcome."

"That's very nice."

A silence ensued while Paul tried to think of an excuse to get off the phone.

"Why don't you check with Leah," Rich suggested. "In case she made other plans."

"Oh . . . right." Paul realized he probably sounded like an idiot. "Hold on a minute." He cupped his hand over the receiver. "It's Rich. He's inviting us out to dinner Saturday evening. Is that a problem?"

"Ah . . . not that I can think of."

"It's fine," he said. "See you Saturday, then." He was hanging up the receiver when Rich stopped him.

"You might be interested in knowing where and what time."

"Oh, right." He opened his bedstand drawer and got a pen, then wrote down the necessary information using the title page of the paperback he was currently reading.

There was a slight hesitation from Rich once he'd finished. "You okay, Paul? You don't sound like yourself."

"I'm fine," he answered as evenly as possible. He hung up with a cursory goodbye and reached for Leah. "Now, where were we?"

Leah liked Jamie, Rich's wife. But until Paul had joined the softball team, she'd only talked to her sister-in-law occasionally. Whenever she did, though, Leah was impressed with Jamie's charm and graciousness. She didn't know her well enough to confide in her, but she hoped someday she would.

Leah needed a friend. Now more than ever. Diane was gone, and she'd drifted away from Linda, whose life had become so different from her own.

It wouldn't surprise Leah to learn that the

Saturday dinner had been Jamie's idea. The two women had seen each other earlier in the week. Jamie had a doctor's appointment and her usual babysitter hadn't been available, so she'd called Leah. Naturally Leah had been happy to watch Bethany.

Bethany had been no trouble, and Jamie had been so grateful. She'd returned from her doctor's appointment beaming with the news of a second pregnancy. Leah hadn't told Paul, not wanting to ruin Rich's surprise.

Perhaps it was Jamie's happy news that brought Diane to mind. Leah missed her sister in so many ways. Yet she couldn't help feeling that Diane still stood between her and Paul. Between her and the children.

Although Paul had been quick to offer her reassurances that Diane's presence hadn't followed them into the bedroom, Leah's fears weren't completely laid to rest. She hoped Paul had told her the truth — that Diane wasn't part of their lovemaking. But if that was the case, why did Leah struggle with so much guilt?

Leah was afraid she knew exactly why. Without ever intending it, she truly had taken her sister's place.

Although the children called her Leah, they thought of her as their mother. As Elizabeth Manning had pointed out, Leah was the only mother Kelsey had ever known.

She was a wife to Paul, too. A wife in every sense. But Leah wasn't fooling herself. She knew her sister was the children's mother. Although he'd married her, Paul didn't love her. Maybe he wanted her, something he confessed to often. Maybe he needed her, something he demonstrated frequently. But he didn't love her. Not the way he had Diane.

Leah had thought she'd be content marrying Paul so she could raise the twins and Kelsey as her own children. A husband and family were more than she'd ever dreamed of having. But, to her dismay, she found herself becoming greedy.

The realization lay heavy on her heart. She'd always be a substitute. A poor second. A stand-in wife and mother.

Perhaps she was just feeling sorry for herself. It wasn't like her to feel so melancholy or morose, but she was carrying an additional burden now. . . .

It didn't make sense that taking her sister's place should suddenly bother Leah so much. Not when she'd been living with Paul for nearly three months, married to him a month of that time.

Admit it, her heart cried. *You're in love with him.*

So what if I am?

He loves Diane.

That's all right, you loved Diane, too. She asked you to take her place, remember?

Leah did remember, but she hadn't expected to fall in love with Paul. Hadn't expected so many things.

She dressed carefully for the Saturday dinner, wanting Paul to be proud of her, but knowing that no matter what she wore or how she did her hair, she'd never be as beautiful as Diane.

Paul was in and out of the bedroom while she dressed. She'd been looking forward to this evening all week. Now she wasn't sure.

She'd been feeling listless all day, tired, a bit despondent. At noon she'd lain down with the kids and napped. Leah couldn't remember the last time she'd taken a nap. Not since she'd moved in with Paul, at any rate.

"You ready?" he asked, walking into the bedroom.

"I will be in a few minutes."

Paul frowned. "Are you feeling all right?"

She nodded, holding back her news. All her life she'd been far too prone to keeping secrets.

"You're not feeling well, are you?"

She sat at the edge of the bed and picked up her shoe, slipping on the patent leather pump. She hadn't meant to say anything, at least not yet.

"Did I tell you I looked after Bethany the other day while Jamie went to the doctor?" she asked, her voice low.

"I remember you said something about it. Why?"

"No reason." She backed off, not wanting to ruin the evening for them both.

"Leah, what's wrong?"

"Nothing." She pressed her fingers under her eyes, afraid she might start weeping. "I've been feeling . . . different all day."

"Any reason?" He sat on the bed beside her and reached for her hand.

Leah shrugged.

"Rich tells me Jamie's expecting again."

Leah nodded. "I'm really happy for them."

"Better them than us," Paul said with a small laugh.

Leah withdrew her hand from his. "What makes you say that?" she asked.

"For obvious reasons."

"I . . . see," she said stiffly.

"What do you see?" He sounded so puzzled.

There was no hiding the truth now. "Did

it ever occur to you that . . . that I might be pregnant, too?"

Ten

"Are you pregnant?" Paul demanded. He couldn't seem to stand still. His heart was in his throat, and the *fear* . . . the all-consuming fear overwhelmed him. He shoved his hands in his pants pockets and formed tight fists.

"*Are* you?" he demanded a second time when Leah didn't respond.

"I don't know. Not for sure. But . . ."

He jerked one hand free and raked it through his hair. "How could something like this have happened?"

Leah looked so small, sitting there on the edge of the bed. His question appeared to revive her. Slowly, her hazel eyes burning with indignation, she stared at him. "What do you mean, how could something like this have happened? Think about it, Paul. Just think about it."

"We've been careful." In fact, he'd taken responsibility for birth control himself.

"What . . . what about the first time?"

He uttered a curse, short and to the point. Then, when he saw Leah flinch, his regret was instantaneous. He would've given his right arm to yank back the ugly word. That first night they'd made love had been one of the most beautiful experiences of his life. But the thought that their first time together might have resulted in pregnancy terrified him to the marrow of his bones.

"There was one other time, too . . . remember?" she informed him quietly.

Paul did remember. He'd been so eager for her they hadn't taken the necessary precautions. "How late are you?" he asked after a moment.

"Six days."

"Oh, no." Diane had never been late, except when she was carrying the twins and Kelsey. She'd always known by the end of the first week of her missed period whether or not she was pregnant.

"I . . . I'm not usually late, but . . . I could be for one reason or another."

Paul nodded, but he wasn't listening as he remembered the past few days. Leah had seemed tired and listless. Diane had been the same way during the first trimester of her pregnancies.

His heart froze in his chest, the dread

nearly devouring him. He *couldn't* lose Leah. Not his wife. Not again. He couldn't bear it; he couldn't survive without Leah. Not now, when he was just beginning to live again.

"I . . . I made an appointment with the doctor for Monday morning," she said haltingly. "I wasn't going to say anything until I'd been to see him . . . but —"

"You should've said something before this," he broke in.

"Why?" she flared. "So you could be angry with me sooner?"

"I'm not angry."

"You're not exactly overjoyed, either."

"You're right," he answered crossly, "I'm not. Can you blame me?"

"No." The word was a strangled whisper. Her chin came up and tears brimmed in her eyes, ready to spill down her ashen cheeks. Her lower lip started to tremble, and Paul felt a knife twist in his heart.

She was so vulnerable, sitting there, pale and beautiful, bleeding from the wounds his fear had inflicted. He knelt in front of her and clasped her hands in his own. Taking a deep breath, he closed his eyes. "I'm sorry, Leah. I didn't mean to upset you. Whatever happens, we'll deal with it together. All right?"

She nodded.

The doorbell chimed in the distance, and Paul knew it was the babysitter. "Are you ready?"

Once more Leah nodded. "I think so . . . I'm sorry, my timing's incredibly bad — I shouldn't have mentioned it tonight. It just sort of . . . slipped out."

Paul kissed her temple and placed his hand on her shoulder. "We'll talk about it later. For now, let's put it aside and enjoy our dinner. Agreed?"

She gave him a watery smile and nodded.

Leah didn't know how she was going to survive dinner with Paul's family.

She desperately wished she hadn't told Paul she might be pregnant. She'd been conscious of the possibility for the past few days, so she'd already gone through the full spectrum of emotions. It hadn't been fair to hit Paul with the news so unexpectedly — just before a dinner party, of all things.

The moment the thought of pregnancy occurred to her, Leah's immediate reaction had been sheer joy. She'd been standing in front of the kitchen calendar when the realization suddenly struck her. It didn't seem possible. So soon? They hadn't made love all that often yet, but it seemed the most logical explanation for why she was late.

Her timing wasn't exactly spectacular — they'd only been married a few weeks — but Leah was thrilled. She loved Paul and the thought of having his baby, *their* baby, had filled her with excitement.

She'd been fearful, too. But not because of her sister. Diane's death had come about through a rare series of events. The likelihood that it might happen again was so slim it didn't warrant consideration. What did concern her were the demands of another child. She loved Kelsey and the twins, but by the end of the day she was exhausted. She was worried, too, about how the children would feel about another sibling.

But her biggest fear of all had been Paul's reaction. For that reason alone, she hadn't intended to mention anything to him until she was certain. She certainly hadn't intended to blurt it out the way she had. Perhaps she was hoping, praying, that he'd share some of her happiness.

Only Paul hadn't been happy. He'd been upset. Then regretful. She could understand and forgive his reaction; nevertheless it hurt. In fact, the pain went so deep, Leah didn't know how she was going to sit through dinner and smile.

"How often have you been late before?" Paul asked when they were in the car.

"Not often, and never more than a few days . . . that I can remember."

His hands tightened on the steering wheel until his knuckles went white. "I was afraid of that."

"I . . . thought you said we shouldn't worry about it now."

He sighed. "You're right, but I don't know if I *can* stop thinking about it."

Leah waited a moment, her heart aching. "Would it be so terrible?"

"Yes." His response was immediate. Harsh.

Leah's throat constricted. She turned her head and looked out the side window, wondering how she was going to keep from crying. It wouldn't hurt nearly as much if she didn't know how Paul had reacted when Diane told him she was pregnant with the twins, or when they'd learned she was going to have Kelsey. Paul had been delighted. Exuberant. He'd been so excited they'd celebrated for weeks. Diane had claimed Paul loved her the most when she was pregnant. He was gentle and romantic.

With Diane.

With Leah he was angry and disappointed.

Unexpectedly Paul reached for her hand,

gripping it tightly. "Don't worry, we'll get through this."

"I'm not the one who's worried."

From the corner of her eye, Leah watched as Paul frowned darkly. "Maybe you should be."

"Why?"

"Why?" he exploded. "You just don't get it, do you? Look what happened to Diane when she had Kelsey. Do you honestly think I want to lose you?"

"A pregnancy isn't going to kill me."

"I don't want to chance it," he said firmly, leaving no room for discussion.

"Unfortunately, we may not have the option."

His lips tightened. "Do you mind if we deal with this some other time? We're nearly at the restaurant."

"All right," she whispered, managing by some miracle to hold the tears at bay.

When they arrived, Jason was sitting in the restaurant foyer waiting for them. Leah could've sworn it was the first time she'd seen Paul's brother without a baseball cap on his head. He was tall and good-looking, his eyes the same intense shade of blue as Paul's. He stood, smiling, when they entered the restaurant.

"Glad you two made it," Jason said. "Rich

and Jamie will be here any minute."

Paul's smile lacked friendliness. He didn't respond to Jason's remark; instead, he buried his hands in his pockets and stared across the linen-covered tables at the view of Lake Union.

"So, Leah," Jason said, apparently willing to try again, "how's married life treating you?"

"Fine." There was no need to exaggerate.

Jason hesitated. "I'm pleased to hear it."

Leah, too, focused her gaze on the distance. The ability to make small talk had deserted her completely.

"Jamie made reservations," Jason announced. "Why don't we wait for them at our table? We might as well relax and enjoy the view."

"Sounds like a good idea to me." Paul said. He placed his hand at the small of Leah's back as they followed the hostess to a table for six by the window.

"Will someone else be joining us?" Leah asked conversationally, hoping to make up for her unsociable behavior earlier. "A date, Jason?"

"Not for me," he said, reaching toward the middle of the table for a bread stick. "I'm leaving all the marrying in this family to everyone else."

"Don't you want to get married?"

"Yes and no . . . I'm not opposed to it if that's how things go, but it isn't in my game plan right now."

"I know what you mean," Leah said, helping herself to an olive, ignoring Paul, who sat silent and morose beside her. "It would be nice if it happened, but if you don't find someone it won't be the end of the world."

"Exactly."

Paul remained ominously silent.

A few minutes later, Rich and Jamie arrived. Jamie's eyes were bright with happiness. Rich pulled out the chair for his wife, his gaze holding hers as they exchanged a lover's look.

They all greeted one another and then they studied the menu. "Tonight's a dual celebration," Rich announced proudly, smiling at his wife. "As you probably know, Jamie and I are going to be parents again."

"All right!" Jason said, pumping his fist in the air.

"Congratulations," Leah said, continuing to study her menu.

"Congratulations," Paul echoed with a decided lack of enthusiasm.

If anyone noticed, and Leah prayed they hadn't, they didn't comment. Watching Rich and Jamie and seeing the love they shared so openly, so generously, with each other, Leah felt her heart ache anew.

She hadn't thought she could have been any more miserable than she already was, but sitting through dinner with Paul's brother and his wife was agony. The love between Rich and Jamie was like a mirror that reflected all the weaknesses in Leah's relationship with Paul. His reaction to the news that she might be pregnant confirmed everything she'd ever feared about her marriage.

They ordered their meals and a bottle of champagne to honor Leah and Paul's wedding. But Leah didn't feel much like celebrating and apparently Paul didn't, either. For the second time that evening, Leah prayed no one noticed. She wasn't worried about Rich and Jamie feeling slighted; their attention was completely on each other. But Jason was another story. More than once she felt her brother-in-law's gaze. She tried to smile, tried to reassure him, but Leah discovered she had very little reassurance to give.

Not once did Paul speak directly to her during dinner. Leah didn't know if the snub was intentional or not. Nor had he spoken to anyone else unless he was addressed, and then he responded with as few words as possible.

The entire evening was a disaster. Leah fully accepted the blame. She should never have told Paul about the baby . . . if there even was a baby.

"You barely touched your dinner," he commented on the drive home.

"I . . . wasn't hungry." And she hadn't taken more than a sip or two of champagne, just in case she *was* pregnant.

After that remark he didn't say anything. He gazed straight ahead, concentrating on the road.

"You didn't seem interested in eating yourself," she said tentatively sometime later.

Still not looking at her, Paul expelled his breath. "I guess I wasn't hungry, either."

That night Paul couldn't sleep. Guilt and fear made for hellish companions in bed. He'd never thought of himself as a particularly heroic man, but he wasn't a coward, either. From the minute Leah announced she might be pregnant, he'd revised that opinion of himself.

He was the biggest coward who ever lived. He'd trembled with fear as soon as the word *pregnant* left her lips.

Knowing it was useless to lie there and toss and turn, Paul climbed out of bed and made his way into the kitchen. He didn't turn on any lights, but pulled out a chair and sat down in the dark. Propping his elbows on the table, he hid his face in his hands as he tried to reason with himself.

He should've been more careful, he told himself. He was an adult. He knew how to prevent a pregnancy. Considering what had happened to Diane, his carelessness, his casual neglect of precautions, horrified him.

He loved Leah, honestly loved her. He didn't understand how he'd been so fortunate as to have married two of the most generous, loving women he'd ever known.

He *couldn't* lose Leah. He didn't have what it took to live through losing her. He couldn't bury another wife.

The memory of the night Diane died came back to him. He recalled Dr. Charman's words as he told Paul how sorry he was, how he'd done everything possible to save her. He'd explained exactly what had gone wrong, but by then Paul hadn't been listening. All he'd heard was that his wife was dead.

A fresh wave of grief washed over him.

He couldn't lose Leah, too. He couldn't!

Not for the first time, Paul realized how

selfish and self-centered he'd been when it came to Leah. Without intending to, he'd slighted her in so many ways.

He was just beginning to deal with her news — her possible pregnancy — just beginning to accept it, face his fears and prepare to speak openly with her, when he'd heard her talking to Jason about marriage. Leah had never expected to marry, she'd told his brother, and hadn't really cared whether it happened or not. She seemed so blasé, so flippant. Her attitude had stunned him.

And yet here he was, crazy in love with her. He'd assumed he was well past the point of having his feelings hurt. Nevertheless, her words *had* hurt him.

Perhaps he was overreacting; Paul didn't know anymore. He loved her, and she'd made their marriage sound like . . . like an accident. Inconsequential. As if she'd only agreed to his proposal because she wasn't likely to get another.

Maybe if he hadn't been so worried about her being pregnant, he might not have taken the comment so personally. Paul wasn't sure about that, either.

His thoughts churned for hours, until dawn crept over the horizon. Somewhere near morning, he returned to bed and crawled between the covers, gathering Leah in his arms, needing her warmth to chase away the chill that had taken hold of his heart.

Monday morning Paul came out of their bedroom dressed for work while Leah was making breakfast for Kelsey and the boys. Ryan and Ronnie were setting the table, and Kelsey was in her high chair, batting her cup against the tray and singing cheerfully.

Not once since they'd left the restaurant on Saturday night had Paul mentioned the possibility of Leah's being pregnant. He didn't need to; it was there between them like a living, breathing thing. He hadn't made love to her, either. Leah didn't know if he intended to ever touch her again.

"What time is your doctor's appointment?" he asked as he poured a cup of coffee.

"Nine."

"I want you to call me."

"At the office?" She'd never called him at the newspaper before.

"Yes. I'll be in all morning."

Waiting for your call. He didn't say it, but he might as well have.

"All right," she said, keeping her back to him.

"I'll talk to you later."

Leah nodded. "Later."

It wasn't until the door closed that she realized he'd left for work. Without kissing her, without even telling the kids goodbye, without saying another word, he'd walked out.

Tears rained down her cheeks; there was no controlling her emotions any longer. She turned off the burner and brought the plate of French toast to the table, where the boys were waiting.

She was grateful that the twins didn't seem to notice she was weeping. She let them dish up their own plates, spread the butter and pour the syrup — half of which ended up on the table.

Rubbing her eyes, she sat down with the boys, but, like Paul, she didn't have much of an appetite. Holding her cup in her hands, she leaned her elbows on the table.

"Leah?"

Ronnie stood beside her chair, his big blue eyes gazing up at her.

"What is it, sweetheart?"

"Here," he said, shoving his tattered yellow blanket into her lap.

Touched by his generosity, Leah hugged him close. It was then that the sobs overtook her.

■ ■ ■ ■

Paul had gone forty-eight hours on less than five hours' sleep. He'd woken feeling as though the two hours he'd slept had made him feel worse than if he hadn't slept at all.

Furthermore he was dangerous in this condition — to himself and to others. He was halfway to work before he realized he'd even left the house. It wouldn't have concerned him so much if he hadn't been driving. He couldn't remember leaving home or saying goodbye to Leah and the children. If he had, the memory had escaped him.

The phone on his desk rang, and Paul grabbed the receiver, dropping it in his anxiety.

"Paul Manning."

"All right, what's going on?" It was Jason.

"What do you mean?"

"Between you and Leah. Dinner Saturday night was supposed to be a celebration."

"It was . . ."

"Not from where I sat," Jason countered.

"Leave it alone," Paul said crisply. He wasn't one to share his problems and never had been. If Leah was pregnant, the news would come out soon enough. There was no reason to discuss it with Jason.

"Not this time, big brother."

"I can't talk," Paul said crossly. "I'm expecting an important call."

"From whom?"

"Leah," Paul said without thinking.

"Do you expect her to phone and apologize?"

Paul laughed. "You aren't going to trick me into discussing my problems, so don't even try."

"I wasn't," Jason denied. "But you admit there *are* problems?" He sighed loudly. "Listen, Paul, would you stop being so almighty proud for once? We're family. You seem to think that just because you're the oldest you should be able to deal with everything all by yourself. Well, I've got news for you, big brother. You aren't any better than the rest of us."

"I never thought I was."

"Then tell me what's wrong with you and Leah. I've hardly ever seen two people look so unhappy."

Paul hesitated and rubbed his face. He was weary in body and spirit. Worried sick. Frightened out of his wits, and he didn't know what to do. Make a counseling appointment, he supposed; spill his guts to a professional.

He pinched the bridge of his nose. "Leah

thinks she might be pregnant," he admitted hoarsely.

"No way!" His voice was shocked. Incredulous. Dismayed.

"My sentiments exactly," Paul said, grateful that his brother understood his fear. Grateful, too, that Jason hadn't made some stupid comment about Paul keeping his pants zipped. They were zipped now. He hadn't touched Leah in two nights. It hadn't helped, either. If anything, it had increased the tension between them.

"When's she going to the doctor?"

"This morning. She said she'd phone me."

"How does she feel about it?"

Paul had to stop and think. Darned if he knew. He'd never stopped to ask her. "I . . . don't know," he said reluctantly.

"What about you?"

"I've never been so frightened in my life! I haven't slept in two nights. . . . The thought of losing Leah . . ."

"You won't."

"How can you be so sure?" he demanded. "Diane gave birth to the twins without much of a problem. Who would've believed a second pregnancy would kill her?"

"Yes, but aren't you forgetting something?"

"What?" Paul asked impatiently.

"Leah."

Paul stopped cold. Jason was right. He'd been so wrapped up in his own fears, he hadn't taken Leah's feelings into consideration. Not even once. If she showed any fear of being pregnant, he hadn't sensed it. But he didn't understand how she could *not* be afraid. He was terrified, and they weren't even certain yet.

"But what?" Jason prompted.

"She doesn't actually seem frightened of being pregnant." If anything, Paul had detected a hint of exhilaration, a joyful expectation. With his own fears running rampant, with his guilt and anxiety, he'd ignored *her* feelings.

"In other words, all Leah knows is that you're scared."

"No." It wasn't until now, talking to his brother, that Paul realized how badly he'd bungled things once again. "All she knows is that I'm angry."

"Angry?"

"Yes, angry."

"With her?"

"No," he said forcefully. "That wouldn't make any sense. I'm furious with myself."

"And she *knows* this?"

"Of course she knows it." Or at least he assumed she did. Assumed that she understood his concern was for her, because he loved her so much.

"You're sure of this?"

Paul rubbed the back of his neck. "You know, Jason, maybe you've missed your calling in life. You should be the reporter, not me."

Jason chuckled and Paul smiled, too. "I can see there's some fence-mending I need to do with my wife. I guess I should thank you for being so kind as to point that out to me."

"Anytime. If I ever get married, which is unlikely, you'll be the one I turn to when I'm in trouble."

"Frankly," Paul said, "I don't think that's such a good idea."

"Why not?"

"Because I've got to be about the worst example of a husband you could find."

"Don't be so hard on yourself. You're only human."

"Would you care to explain that to Leah for me?"

"Not on your life. That, big brother, is something you'll have to do."

"That's what I thought you'd say."

It wasn't easy, but with a little begging and a lot of bargaining, Paul managed to get the rest of the day off. What he had to say to Leah couldn't be said over the phone, nor could it wait. He'd been so wrapped up in himself and his own fears that he'd hurt the one person in the world — besides his children — whose happiness meant everything to him.

He drove home, parked in the driveway and leapt out of the car. He raced into the kitchen to find Leah folding laundry. He stopped abruptly.

"I . . . I tried to phone the office twice," she told him quietly. "They said you weren't there. Your cell was off. I left messages."

Now that he was home, with his wife, Paul found himself at a loss for words. He held out his arms to her. "I did try to phone," she said again. "There was no reason for you to rush home."

"Don't say anything else."

She looked at him as though she wasn't sure what to expect. He enclosed her in his arms, cherishing her warmth, her softness.

Holding her face between his hands, he gazed down on her. Her puffy eyes told him she'd been crying. It broke his heart to acknowledge that he was the source of her grief.

"Leah," he said, then paused, not knowing how to proceed. Showing her how he felt seemed easier. He loved her, and it was time she knew it. He kissed her hungrily, deeply, his mouth moving over hers with a desperation that verged on wild. "I love you, Leah," he chanted. "I love you. I love you."

"Paul . . . I'm not . . ." She tried to break away from him, and he felt the resistance in her. He knew he'd won whatever battle she was waging when she parted her lips to him.

Leah broke away and hid her face in his chest, her shoulders heaving. "Why tell me that now?" she asked.

"Because it's true . . . because I should've told you before. I've been so worried you might be pregnant and —"

"I'm not."

"You're not?"

"The doctor said he doesn't know why my period's so late. It probably has something to do with anxiety, but I can't recall being upset about anything."

The relief that flowed through Paul felt like water on a parched garden. He tried not to show it, not to reveal how grateful he was that he didn't have to face this fear head-on so soon after their marriage. So soon after he'd found happiness again.

"You'll be happy to hear something else."

"What's that?"

"I'm not going to get pregnant, either . . . I'm going on the pill, so you won't need to worry about me getting pregnant with a baby you don't want."

Eleven

"It isn't that I don't want another child," Paul started to explain, but Leah turned away, not wanting to hear. She picked up a towel and held it protectively against her stomach.

"Paul, I know what your feelings were. Please don't try to sugarcoat them now. You could barely look at me. . . . You haven't touched me since . . . Friday night. This morning you left for work without bothering to say goodbye — as though you couldn't wait to get away from me."

"Leah, it's not what you think." His hands settled on her shoulders, but when she stiffened he released her. He walked around the table so she wouldn't have any choice but to look at him, although she still avoided eye contact.

"What else was there for me to think?" she asked. "That you'd be overjoyed if I got pregnant? That you'd arrange for someone to take the children so we could celebrate alone? Did you arrive home with my favorite ice cream and a jar of pickles?"

Her words had the desired effect. He went pale. It was how Diane and Paul had celebrated when they'd learned Diane was pregnant with Kelsey. Alone, their happiness bubbling over, their love and excitement centered on each other.

"I got the message, Paul. Loud and clear."

"It's just that I was so afraid of losing you. . . ."

"Exactly. Who'd be here to wash and clean for you? Who'd be here to raise your children and . . . and warm your bed?" she added scornfully. "You'd miss me, all right, but for all the wrong reasons."

"Leah . . . no! It isn't like that. I love you."

"I saw how much you love me." She threw the towel she was folding down on the table and walked into the backyard. Her garden was in full bloom, the tomato plants heavy with reddening fruit. Now that summer was ending, her small harvest was almost ready to reap. Colorful sheets from the twins' beds were on the line she'd asked him to put up, flapping in the wind. On days like this, she hung laundry outside to dry, both to cut down on the electricity she used, and for the clean, breezy smell. The evidence of her life here was all around her.

Leah stood with her back to the house and brushed the tears from her eyes. She heard the door close, alerting her that Paul had followed her outside.

"I may have cheated you in a lot of ways," he admitted, his words deceptively soft. "You didn't have the courtship you deserved or even the wedding you should've had. There are probably countless other ways in which you've lost out in this marriage. But I never intended it to be like this — I never meant to be so thoughtless and self-centered."

A long moment passed. "I love you, Leah. I know you don't believe me. I can't blame you for that, but it's the truth." The words echoed with pain and regret. "What can I do?"

"Do?"

"To right the wrongs . . . to prove to you I mean what I say. To make up for the way I acted when I thought you might be pregnant."

Leah didn't know. Even if she could have, there was nothing she'd change. She'd moved into his home voluntarily. Married him of her own free will. She loved the children, loved being their mother, and, God help her, she loved Paul, too. With all her heart and soul, she loved Paul.

"Tell me, and whatever you want me to, I'll do."

"It's not that simple."

"I know."

She turned to face him then, her heart hammering. But when she tried to speak, the words refused to come out. "Just . . ."

"Yes?" He moved one step closer to her. One small step.

"Just . . . love me . . ."

"I do. Oh, Leah, I do." He reached for her, burying his face in the curve of her shoulder, his body shuddering against hers.

". . . the same way you loved Diane."

"How does it feel to have the boys in kindergarten half days?" Jamie Manning asked Leah. It was the second week of September, and they were shopping at the mall, pushing their strollers side by side down the concourse, checking out the fall sales.

"They love it."

"What about you?"

"The truth?" Leah said, smiling at her sister-in-law. "I love it, too."

"Free at last," Jamie cried dramatically, then, glancing down at Kelsey, amended the statement. "Well, almost free."

"I can't believe how much more time I have with the boys gone in the mornings. Wait until Bethany starts preschool and you'll know what I mean."

Jamie paused as they neared the food court. "Dare we stay for an early lunch?"

Leah checked her watch. "Depends on how brave you feel."

"Oh, I've always been pretty brave."

"Be warned — Kelsey likes to throw food."

"No problem. We'll sit as far away from other people as we can."

Leah agreed. It felt good to get out of the house for a while, although shopping had never excited her much before. But now that she had Paul and the children to buy for, she enjoyed it.

Taking a morning off to spend with Jamie had lifted her spirits. During the past couple of weeks, things had been strained between her and Paul. He was trying hard to please her, but instead of helping, it had only made matters worse. The harder he tried to prove his love for her, the more forced it seemed. Paul was in a no-win situation, and Leah had put him there.

Leah needed a confidante. A friend. Jamie was fast becoming both.

Leah bought a chicken salad and for

Kelsey, an order of french fries. She'd prepare a proper lunch when they got home. Jamie got a slice of pizza for herself and bread sticks for Bethany. In a few minutes they had the toddlers in high chairs the mall provided and were sitting at a small table as far from the other diners as they could get.

"By the way," Jamie said, looking at Leah's watch, "is that new?"

She nodded, swallowing a bite of her salad. "Paul got it for me. I casually mentioned how much I like Mickey Mouse and the very next day he brought me this."

"Your birthday?"

"No." Leah set aside her plastic fork and lowered her head. "He . . . he feels guilty."

"Guilty? Why?"

She shrugged. "We . . . thought I was pregnant not long ago. Paul doesn't want another baby. I know a big part of what he was feeling had to do with what happened to my sister, but at the same time I was terribly hurt by how he acted."

Jamie put down her pizza and nodded. "We have a lot in common, Leah, more than you realize. Rich and I didn't come into our marriage in the typical way, either. In fact, we made arrangements for a divorce when we planned the wedding."

Leah knew the gist of Jamie and Rich's

marriage story, but not the details. "You married Rich because you wanted a baby, isn't that right?"

Jamie smiled and smoothed the soft blond curls from her daughter's forehead. "Something like that. I wanted a baby, and because I didn't intend to marry, I asked Rich to be the father. It made sense to me, since I wasn't in love with him. Oh, I mean, I *was* in love with him, only I didn't realize it at the time. I told myself he should be Bethany's father because he had the right genetic makeup." She paused and laughed. "We'd been friends since high school and I approached him on that basis. Friend to friend. I wanted him to be my sperm donor."

"And he agreed to this?" It didn't sound like the Rich Leah had come to know.

"He insisted, for a variety of reasons, that we get married. I wasn't keen on the idea, but I went along with it because otherwise Rich wouldn't agree to my plan."

"Then Bethany was conceived artificially?"

Jamie laughed once more. "No, she was conceived the good old-fashioned way. The same way this baby was." She flattened her hand against her abdomen. "So you see, I wasn't exactly a traditional bride, either."

"I imagine you and Rich thought Paul was crazy to marry me."

"No," Jamie said emphatically. "The situation's unusual, but no more than ours. You've been so good for Paul, good for the children, too." She hesitated. "Do you love him?"

"Yes." Leah's whole heart went into that word.

"I knew you did. He loves you, too."

Leah dropped her gaze. She wasn't nearly as confident of Paul's feelings as her own. He needed her, but she'd always wonder if he truly loved her. For herself. For Leah, the shy, plain Baker sister. The plodding math teacher with her logical mind.

When he'd told her he loved her that morning two weeks earlier, it had seemed like a miracle. She realized now it was the only thing he could say under the circumstances, knowing how badly he'd hurt her. He was seeking a way to atone for the pain he'd unwittingly inflicted. Leah wanted to believe him so badly. He had touched a chord in her she hadn't known existed, satisfied a craving that reached far back into her childhood. In all her life, no man had ever really loved her. Not her father, who'd abandoned her when she was barely old enough to remember him. Not Rob. Not the few other men she'd dated. It seemed obvious to her that whatever a woman needed to make a man happy, Leah Baker lacked.

Until Paul. He made her vulnerable in ways she'd never experienced. Vulnerable to love. Vulnerable to a happiness she'd never expected to find. Vulnerable to a tenderness that touched her heart.

"He's trying so hard," Leah whispered. Trying to give her all the things she'd missed before their marriage. In the past two weeks, he'd resumed his courting, with gifts and compliments. He'd wooed her back into his bed and loved her with an urgency that melted any resistance.

He was trying so hard . . . to love her, for herself.

"Rich and I experienced our own problems," Jamie went on to say. "We never intended there to be anything physical between us. It was supposed to have been a marriage of convenience — but it turned out to be one of *in*convenience."

"What happened?"

Jamie took a sip of her soft drink before answering. "We were secretly married, and I had dinner with a former boyfriend. It wasn't a date, wasn't even close to one. He was married and having problems and needed someone to listen to him."

"Rich was jealous?"

"Terribly. But to be fair to Rich, his feelings were understandable. The woman he'd recently broken up with had been cheating on him, and it seemed to Rich that I was doing the same thing. Everything blew up in our faces."

"But it all worked out, didn't it?"

"Eventually, but things got worse before they got better." Jamie's hand tightened around her soft drink. "I guess what I'm trying to say is, I don't want you to be discouraged. I've known Paul for quite a few years. He's an honorable man. I can't believe he'd ever have married you if he didn't truly love you. If you're having problems now, don't worry about it. All couples do. There's a period of adjustment." Jamie grimaced comically. "I sound like I really know what I'm talking about, don't I?"

Leah smiled. "I appreciate hearing it, but even more than that, I appreciate having someone to talk to. . . . I miss Diane so much. I not only lost my sister — I lost my best friend."

"Paul understands that," Jamie said quietly. "Diane was his best friend, too."

■ ■ ■ ■

It was Friday night. Late Friday night. Leah sat up in bed reading, and Paul was working feverishly on his novel, writing the last chapter. A marathon session. Leah decided she'd wait for him, which wasn't difficult since she was involved in a whodunit by one of her favorite authors.

After an exciting chase scene, the book reached its satisfying conclusion. Closing it with a sigh, Leah climbed out of bed and walked into the kitchen, looking for a snack. Something other than graham crackers and peanut butter. She was bending over the lower shelf of the refrigerator when Paul spoke from behind her.

"Now that's an inviting pose."

"Paul," she chided, straightening quickly, a chicken leg clutched in one hand. She shut the refrigerator door and turned around. "So, are you finished?"

He nodded.

"Are you going to let me read it?"

He crossed his arms and leaned against the door frame. "That depends."

"On what?" she asked suspiciously, narrowing her eyes.

"On how much you appreciate literary

genius."

"Oh, I appreciate genius, all right." Paul seemed more relaxed than she'd seen him in weeks. She enjoyed bantering with him, enjoyed his lighthearted mood.

"Might I suggest you lose that chicken leg and come over here?" He held out his arms to her.

Leah gave up her snack to move willingly into his embrace.

His arms slipped around her waist as he lifted her from the floor. "It's taken me nearly two years to get this book on paper."

"But you did it, Paul! You did it."

"I believe a reward would be fitting, don't you?" His gaze focused on her lips.

"What kind of reward?" she asked, batting her lashes in exaggerated enticement.

His eyes darkened in unspoken invitation. "I have a feeling you'll think of something."

"I'm thinking, all right." And she was.

Paul stared into the night, his arms around his wife, feeling utterly content, utterly satisfied. They'd made love for hours. . . .

The urgency he felt to be with Leah hadn't changed in the weeks since their marriage. He didn't understand it, but he'd given up questioning his need for her. It was just there. Powerful and intense.

He'd worked harder these past two weeks at controlling it, for fear she'd accuse him of using her. Maybe on some deep, psychological level he feared it himself. So he was rationing himself. They'd make love once a week — that was all.

Maybe twice, he amended; no need to be stingy. No need to raise Leah's concern should she notice. Yes, twice a week made more sense. Wednesdays and Saturdays. Maybe Monday and Thursdays and either Saturday or Sunday. No, that was three.

Oh, what the heck, three times a week wouldn't be too much. Would it?

He smiled to himself as she nestled her head against his chest. He hadn't slept yet, and it would soon be morning. Close to the time the twins and Kelsey would be waking up.

He didn't care how little sleep he got; tonight had been worth every second of lost sleep. When he'd last looked at the clock, it had been past four. Leah had retrieved her chicken leg and brought it to bed, claiming she was hungry. Who wouldn't be after what they'd just done?

She couldn't let her hunger go unattended, she'd said, attacking the leg. A college professor — even one on sabbatical — couldn't live on love alone. He smiled at the memory.

His book was finished. After two long years, he finally had the story completely worked out. There'd been a sense of fulfillment, an overwhelming sense of accomplishment and pride as he printed out the last chapter. He'd read it over during the next week, do what editing he could at this stage and then mail it off to New York. He'd queried a reputable agent, who'd expressed interest in seeing it. Then the waiting would begin.

Paul was beginning to feel a cautious optimism about life. He was happy. Not *almost* happy. Just plain happy. Once he realized that, he wondered if he should be feeling that way. No, he decided, stopping that train of thought before it could gather speed. He wasn't going to censure himself. He wasn't going to examine his joy under a microscope and punish himself for feeling alive.

He had loved Diane. Loved her now. She'd been his first real love, his first wife, the mother of his children. But she was in the past. She'd always be a part of him. But she was gone.

Then he'd found Leah. She was his heart now. His soul. His joy.

After the mistakes he'd made during the

first few weeks of their marriage, he'd done everything he could to make it up to her, to show her how much he cared. In his own way, on a limited budget, with limited time, he'd been courting her.

Leah was the one who'd brought happiness back to his life. He could laugh again. The grief that had weighed him down for so many months had receded into the background. It no longer dominated his very existence. He still loved Diane and mourned her, but there were other emotions in his life now. Other diversions. He'd been freed from the stranglehold of his grief. His senses were fine-tuned. More poignant. More intense than before.

It was as if he'd woken up one morning and found himself alive after crawling into a grave.

When had it happened? Paul didn't know, but he was sure it had started when Leah decided to move in with him and the children. His whole world had taken a one-hundred-and-eighty-degree turn for the better that day.

They'd had their problems, but then all couples did. Leah was trying to make their marriage work, too. Slowly, as he gained her trust, she was lowering the walls she'd raised. He was winning her confidence bit by bit.

Leah wasn't Diane. She was more sensitive. Less open. A little more guarded, but he was learning. He was learning.

His eyes drifted shut. He was ready to sleep.

He dreamed of her that night.

Diane.

He'd fallen into a deep, contented sleep, and woke with a sick feeling in the pit of his stomach. A feeling of deep loss and sorrow, of regret.

Try as he might, Paul couldn't remember the details of the dream, only that it had been about Diane. He sat up in bed and held his head between his hands, feeling as though he had a terrible hangover.

Why did he have this dream *now?* It made no sense. He'd set everything in order, made his resolutions, chosen life. Chosen love.

Leah was awake. He could hear her in the kitchen with the children. He staggered out of bed and threw on yesterday's clothes.

Kelsey was sitting in her high chair waving a spoon, while the boys were stationed in front of the television set, watching Saturday-morning cartoons. Leah stood by the kitchen sink, sipping from a cup of coffee. All around him were the signs of ordinary life. Everyday, ordinary, *wonderful* life.

"Morning," he said. "You should've woken me."

Leah didn't answer.

"Leah?" He reached for a mug and poured himself a cup of coffee. She kept her back to him.

"Is something wrong?"

She shook her head and set her cup aside before walking down the hallway to the bedroom.

He took a minute to drink some coffee, unclog his mind, before he followed her. She was sitting on the end of the bed, looking lost and small and vulnerable.

He sat next to her, his stomach twisted in tight knots, dread filling his mouth. "What happened?"

"Nothing."

"Leah, don't play games with me," he said sharply. "Obviously something's upset you. Tell me what it is."

She was holding a tissue in her hand and had wound it around her index finger several times. "You . . . were asleep."

"The dream." It came to him with sudden clarity. "Did I call you Diane?"

Leah nodded.

"I . . . I had a dream. I don't know why, I just did. That's the thing about dreams — you don't control them. She was in it, which is about all I remember." He paused. "I'm sorry, Leah, but I swear to you that I didn't intentionally call you by her name."

"I know that."

"All I can do is ask you to forgive me."

"It isn't you who needs to be forgiven."

Paul closed his eyes, weary to the bone. "What do you want me to do? Tell me."

"I can't kid myself any longer, Paul."

"Kid yourself?"

"Diane was my sister, I loved her . . . she was my best friend from the time we were children. Even though she was younger, she was better than me in every area except grades. She was bright and pretty and fun. I was dull and plain and boring."

"Leah!"

"No, let me finish. Please, let me finish while I have the courage. I never competed with her, never allowed myself to be put in that position, because I knew, I always *knew,* I'd be the loser. The problem isn't you, Paul, it's me."

"I don't understand."

"I've discovered I'm greedy and jealous and I hate myself for it. I hate thinking the things I do. I hate feeling sick with envy

247

because you love Diane. I feel guilty and miserable and I can't go on like this."

"Leah, Diane's gone. I've let her go — released her. She's my past. You're my present, my future."

"I wish it was that simple," she said with a sob.

"You don't need to compete with her."

Leah turned to look at him, her gaze unflinching. "Do you love her?"

He didn't hesitate. "Yes, but I love you, too."

"I need some time . . . to think, sort out my feelings. I'm sorry. . . ."

"Time?" He went cold with fear. She was going to leave him. His heart was in turmoil, his head spinning. Could he have found happiness only to lose it again?

"I . . . can't sleep with you anymore, Paul. You want me, you desire me, but it's Diane you love. It's Diane you call for in the middle of night. Not me. For the first time in my life, I'm not willing to take second place to my sister. For once, just this once, I want something just for me. I want to be loved for *me.*"

She started to cry then, and Paul knew that nothing he could say would comfort her.

TWELVE

Paul drove around for several hours, trying to clear his head. A light rain had begun and the skies were gray, which only depressed him more. He parked his car when he passed the small apartment complex his brother Jason owned. He sat there, wondering if he should talk to his younger brother.

He never discussed his problems with anyone, not even family. Generally he preferred to work things out by himself, without the counsel of relatives or friends.

But Jason had said something recently that had struck a chord with Paul. His brother had said it was time Paul realized he wasn't any better than the rest of them — that he should quit being so arrogant.

His brother's assessment had taken Paul by surprise. Jason and Rich viewed him as pompous! He'd thought he was just being strong.

Not dragging out his troubles for others

to analyze wasn't a matter of pride, Paul had reasoned. More a question of habit. He was the oldest in a family of five. The others looked up to him. He was their role model. He could almost hear his parents' words, often repeated, reminding him how important it was to be a good example to the others.

He'd gotten so accustomed to keeping his worries to himself that he wasn't sure he knew *how* to ask for help. Or even if he should.

After several minutes, Paul climbed out of the car and ran toward Jason's apartment. He'd assumed Jason had made a mistake when he'd recently bought the eight-unit complex. As far as he was concerned, renters were nothing but trouble. But his brother didn't seem to be having much of a problem. He managed the building himself, made sure he got the right tenants, then sat back and collected the rent money every month.

Jason answered the door, wearing a football jersey and a baseball cap. He'd been a sports fanatic since they were kids. He'd been on the varsity cross-country, track and swim teams in high school, and he'd continued with cross-country in college.

These days all Jason played was softball,

and the season had ended a couple of weeks earlier. But he still loved to watch any kind of sport.

"Paul!" He sounded surprised to see him.

"Morning."

"It's afternoon."

Paul checked his watch, shocked to see that his brother was right. "So it is."

"Come on in out of the rain. Notre Dame's about to kick off." He motioned toward his sofa, where a bag of potato chips had spilled across the coffee table and a can of soda was sitting on the morning paper.

Paul had only been to Jason's home once before, shortly after his brother had bought the building. A look around told him Jason wasn't much of a housekeeper. Newspapers, at least a week's worth, were carelessly scattered across the beige carpet. A partial load of laundry, towels it looked like, was heaped on the recliner. Several glasses, plates and eating utensils littered the living room.

Jason plopped himself down in front of the television. "Make yourself at home."

Paul sat on the sofa beside him and for a while pretended to pay attention to the game.

"You want something to eat?"

"No, thanks," Paul said. He reached for a potato chip and munched on it before he realized what he was doing.

"So things aren't working out between you and Leah?" Jason asked in that easygoing manner of his.

"How'd you know?" He hated the fact that his younger brother could read him so well. Paul had always thought of himself as aloof, adept at hiding his emotions. Apparently he wasn't as good at it as he'd assumed.

"You got the look, big brother," Jason said, grinning.

"The look?" Paul frowned.

"Yeah, the look of guilt. What'd you do this time?"

"Why are you so sure it was me?" Paul muttered.

" 'Cause it usually is the guy," Jason said without taking his eyes off the television screen.

"For not being married, you certainly seem to be an expert on this." Paul almost wished he'd gone to Rich, instead. He knew Leah had gone shopping with Jamie earlier in the week and he was delighted the two of them had become friends. If he was going to spill his guts, Rich was, for a number of reasons, the more logical choice, yet it was Jason he'd turned to.

"You're right, you know. I *am* guilty."

"You want to talk about it?"

Paul nodded and rubbed his palms together as he gathered his thoughts.

Jason reached for the remote and turned off the TV. "You want a drink? Soda? Beer? Coffee?"

With so many other things on his mind, Paul found making even a simple decision almost impossible. "Coffee, I guess." He followed his brother into the kitchen and marveled that there were any clean dishes left in the house. Dirty pots and pans lined the sink and counter. Ah, the joys of the bachelor life.

Jason opened the dishwasher and pulled out a mug. He examined it before filling it with tap water. Then he opened the microwave, removed a pair of socks and set the mug inside.

While the water was heating, Paul paced the small kitchen. "I had a dream last night . . . about Diane." He paused, half expecting Jason to comment. When his brother didn't, he continued. "I don't remember anything about the dream — only that she was in it."

"Has this happened before?"

"Not that I recall." Paul hardly ever remembered his dreams. "I don't understand it. If Diane was going to haunt my sleep, why now? Why would she come back just when I've made my peace with her death? It doesn't make any sense."

Jason apparently didn't have any answers for him, either.

"I've remarried and after almost a year, I can finally say I'm happy. Leah and I are . . . were," he amended sadly, "working everything out. I've been doing my best to be a good husband, to make up for the things I didn't do earlier. Now *this*."

"Don't go hitting yourself over the head because of a dream."

"It was more than that," Paul admitted sheepishly. "Last night, Leah and I —" he hesitated "— I don't know how to explain it. It was as though for the first time all the barriers were down. I'd finished my novel and —"

"Congratulations!" Jason said.

Paul smiled weakly. "Thanks." He wasn't as excited as he had been. The book, or at least the first draft, was finished, but the exhilaration was gone. Nothing was more important to him than his relationship with his wife.

"Leah and I made love and . . . I don't know how to describe it, Jase, it was so . . . beautiful. I held her in my arms and I realized how much my life had changed since

I married her.

"I feel so whole again. I loved Diane and I always will, but she's gone and I'm alive, and for the first time since I buried her, I'm not sorry to be."

"You've come a long way, Paul."

Paul shook his head. "When I went to sleep I was at peace with myself and my world, and then I had that dream. . . ."

"Did it occur to you that maybe Diane was saying goodbye to you?" Jason asked softly.

"Saying goodbye to me? I don't understand."

"You just finished telling me you'd accepted her death."

"Yes."

"Perhaps your subconscious allowed her the opportunity to release you, too. After Kelsey was born — before Diane died — there wasn't much of a chance for the two of you to talk, was there?"

"No. It happened so fast. Within days she was gone."

"I know." Jason's eyes were somber.

"I wish I remembered more of the dream," Paul said after a moment's silence. "There's a glimmer, but . . . Maybe it'll come back to me."

"Does it really matter?"

Paul pulled out a kitchen chair and sat down. The burden of his guilt had never felt heavier. "There's more. I don't know how it happened, but apparently at some point during the night I called Leah *Diane*."

"You didn't do it on purpose," Jason said. "Surely Leah understands that."

"I don't know what she understands. She was crying and, to be truthful, she wasn't making a whole lot of sense. She kept saying she wouldn't compete with Diane anymore, and that she's moving out of our bedroom because I loved Diane. I'm not supposed to have loved her?" he demanded. "She was my wife!"

"Give Leah time. She's obviously upset, and when you think about it, you can't really blame her."

"As a matter of fact, I'm upset, too," Paul said heatedly. "Where does this leave me? I'm supposed to tell Leah I don't love Diane anymore?"

"She wouldn't believe you even if you did."

"I know," Paul admitted, slumping forward in his chair. "I remember the day I married Diane. It's clear as anything, but it seems like a hundred years ago now. I recall thinking I was going to love this woman all my life. And the amazing part is, I *will* always love her. I can't stop loving her. But I don't understand how it's possible to love two women so intensely."

"You love Leah, too, then?"

Paul nodded. "I didn't go into this marriage with the same rosy vision I did when I married Diane. It made sense to marry Leah. It was a practical decision. I have to admit I was attracted to her, though. I admired and respected her, and she didn't object. But I didn't truly love her when we got married, not the way I loved Diane."

"But now you do. That means something, doesn't it?"

"Apparently not a lot," he answered vehemently. Then he sighed. "I didn't know I could love both of them so much. I struggled with that, thinking I was cheating one or the other." It was a moment of self-realization for Paul; talking to his brother like this was helping him clarify his feelings.

Jason didn't say much, but he sat down across from him.

"Leah and I didn't start our physical relationship right away," Paul continued, a bit chagrined to be discussing his sex life with his unmarried brother. "Neither of us was ready for it."

"At least you were wise enough to recognize that. Not everyone would have."

"For a while I felt like I was being unfaithful to Diane, to Diane's memory, by loving Leah. But try as I might, I couldn't make myself *not* love her."

"She's your wife," he said simply. "You should love her."

In his heart Paul knew Leah was as miserable as he was. He'd tried to talk to her that morning, tried to reason with her, but she was beyond listening. Not knowing what else to say or do, Paul had slipped out of the house.

He'd felt numb as he drove around. Numbness frightened him. For the first few days after Diane's death he'd experienced the same lack of emotion. Gradually, a red-hot pain had overtaken him, and the grief had dominated his every waking moment. The agony had been so consuming that his mind had blotted out whole weeks. He'd functioned, gone to work, taken care of his children, lived day to day, but he didn't remember much of what had happened.

It had all started with a numbness, the same numbness he'd felt that morning when Leah told him he'd called her by her sister's name.

"What are you going to do?" Jason asked him.

Paul had to pull his thoughts together,

mull over his dilemma. "I don't know yet," he said honestly. "Try to rebuild her trust. I'll love her without making any demands on her, give her the space and time she needs."

"Sounds like a good place to start."

Paul smiled. He never did get the cup of coffee his brother had promised him — not that it seemed very palatable. It didn't matter, though. He was finished — or rather he'd found a place to start.

"How'd you get to be so smart?" he asked Jason.

His brother grinned. "Guess it just runs in the family."

Eager now to go home to Leah, Paul left his brother's apartment. He was ready to talk to her, to explain everything he'd realized when he was talking to Jason.

More than anything, he longed to take her in his arms and tell her how much he loved her, how much he needed her, how much he wanted her.

He parked in the driveway and nearly leapt out of the car. He dashed to the front door, throwing it open.

"Leah." Her name was on his lips even before he entered the house.

No response. He hurried into the kitchen to find Kelsey standing up, holding on to the seat of a chair. She gave him a four-toothed smile and thrashed her free arm about with excitement.

A neighbor girl, Angie somebody, was slicing a banana at the counter.

"Oh, hi," she said, smiling broadly.

"Where's Leah?"

"She left about an hour ago."

"Did she say where she was going?"

"No. I'm sorry, I didn't ask. She gave me the phone number to . . ." She reached for a slip of paper. "Here it is, Jamie and Rich's."

"Yes?" Paul prompted.

"She wasn't sure when you'd be back, so she said I should call Jamie if you weren't here by dinnertime. Apparently Jamie was going to come over and pick up the kids."

Paul's heart was pounding. "Did she tell you when she's coming back?"

Angie shook her head. "I don't think it's anytime soon. She must've been going on a trip or something because she took a suitcase with her."

Leah had no business being behind the wheel of a car and she knew it. Tears streamed down her face, blurring her vision, making her a hazard on the road.

She stopped when she came to a red light

260

and blew her nose, then ran the back of her hand across her eyes. The rain that spattered her windshield was the perfect accompaniment to her mood.

She didn't know where she was going, only that she had to get away. The logical thing to do was to check into a hotel. She had to sort through her emotions, try to make sense of why she'd said what she had to Paul. She needed to understand what was going on between her and Paul. Between her and Diane.

Finding somewhere to spend the night might have been rational, but Leah was in no frame of mind for rational behavior. If she had been, she would never have done anything as stupid as packing her bag and walking out on Paul and the children.

But he'd left *her.* He'd left the house, and she'd been all alone with her pain. Everything was crowding in on her, and she'd felt the overwhelming urge to escape.

Leah hated what was happening to her. What was happening to Paul. She'd reacted in anger, lashing back at him for the pain he'd caused her. The same pain she'd carried most of her life, standing on the sidelines while her mother fawned over Diane. She'd smiled and swallowed back the hurt when it was Diane who received new clothes at the beginning of the school year while Leah got hand-me-downs from neighbors and friends.

She'd carried the hurt with her all those years, and yet she loved her sister. Diane couldn't be blamed for being pretty and sweet, any more than Leah could for being plain and serious.

Then Diane had died and, ironic as it seemed, *wrong* as it seemed, that had given Leah a chance at happiness. She'd jealously guarded her heart for so many years. If she was going to fall in love, why did it have to be with her dead sister's husband?

Paul had adored Diane. He still adored her. It didn't seem fair that the only man Leah had ever loved had to be a man who loved her sister so completely.

They were very different, Leah and Diane. Leah could never hope to gain Paul's devotion. He loved her, Leah realized that, but what he felt for her paled in comparison to the depth of his love for Diane.

Once again, she stood in her sister's shadow.

She was jealous of Diane, but why now, when she'd never been jealous before? Early in life she'd accepted her lot, understood her place. So why now? Why, after Diane was gone, did Leah feel this way? It was crazy. *Unfair.*

Leah continued driving in the rain, taking side streets and staying off the busy thoroughfares. Her aimless route led her past a golf course. Golfers carrying umbrellas ambled from one green to another.

With a jolt, it came to her then. She needed to talk to Diane, and even if it was a one-sided conversation, Leah had things that had to be said.

Because she didn't know what street she was on, it took her some time to locate the cemetery. She parked, then walked slowly across the damp lawn, ignoring the drizzle that still hadn't let up.

Nearly a year had passed since Diane's death. In all that time Leah hadn't once visited her sister's grave. She'd stood there as the coffin was lowered — her heart breaking, her breath coming in tortured gasps — and had no desire to ever return.

Paul came often, or he had in the beginning. For months he'd brought fresh flowers each and every week. Leah knew because she'd often looked after the children while he was gone. Sometimes he'd be away for hours; other days it would only be a short while.

Leah couldn't recall the last time he'd

come here. If he still came as often, he hadn't mentioned it to her. Leah wandered around, ignoring the drizzle, searching for her sister's marker.

Diane Sandra Manning, Wife, Mother. The dates of her birth and death were listed along with a Scripture verse from Proverbs 31.

So few words.

Yet they said so much.

She stood looking down at the headstone. An overwhelming sense of sadness came at her and fresh tears filled her eyes, mingling with the rain.

After several minutes, she composed herself enough to speak. "Hi, Sis," she said when she could, her voice tight. "I bet you're surprised I came to see you."

It was probably foolish talking to a patch of lawn. In her heart Leah knew Diane wasn't there; she knew her sister would never hear the words she spoke. But none of that mattered to Leah.

"The boys started kindergarten. Oh, Diane, you'd be so proud of them! They're growing up so fast. Ryan came home from class last week and announced that anyone who could read five whole words didn't need a blankie. He gave it to me and hasn't asked for it even once. Ronnie's given up his thumb, too." She smiled as she smeared the tears across her cheeks.

She began again. "Kelsey's such a precious baby. She's walking now. Three and four steps at a time — she's so eager to get into everything. She's drinking out of a cup, too, but she still has two bottles a day." Leah folded her arms around her waist. "She has your coloring. Her hair's so blond it's white. She's a beautiful little girl."

Leah opened her purse and took out a fresh tissue, which she wadded up in her hand. "Paul finished his novel the other night," she said haltingly.

Then, squaring her shoulders, she closed her eyes. "I love him, too," she cried. "Is that what you wanted — for me to love Paul? I didn't mean for it to happen. . . . I'm not even sure when it did. One morning I woke up and I realized it was too late — I realized I love him.

"What do you want me to do, Diane? I can't fight you for him. We can't sit down and talk this out the way we did when we were teenagers. You can't hug me and tell me everything's okay." She took a deep, shuddering breath. "Paul is your husband. But now he's my husband, too. Is that what you intended? Is it what you wanted? For me to raise your children and . . . and to

265

love Paul?" She was sobbing so hard now, she could barely speak. "Because . . . that's what happened and I feel so wretched."

Suddenly, unexpectedly, it stopped raining. The dark heavy clouds that had blanketed the sky most of the day parted, and a dazzling display of sunlight broke through, shining on the grass, making it glisten.

Leah looked up at the sky, feeling the sun's warmth seep into her bones.

Paul tried to keep the panic at bay as he called Rich's number.

"Hello."

His sister-in-law picked up the phone — for which Paul was grateful. "Jamie, it's Paul," he said, managing to keep his voice smooth. "I just got home. I don't suppose you've heard from Leah?"

"Oh, hi, Paul. No, I haven't. At least not since she phoned this morning."

"Did she say where she was going?"

Jamie didn't hesitate. Paul was listening carefully, waiting for the slightest pause, hoping he wouldn't detect one so he'd know she was telling the truth.

"No, she didn't. Is everything all right? You seem worried."

"Everything's fine," he said abruptly, far more interested in getting the information

he needed than in providing polite reassurances. "How did she sound when she
talked to you?"

"About the same way you're sounding
now. You're *sure* everything's all right?"

"Yes. What did she say?" he asked again.

"Not much. She phoned to ask if I could
take the twins and Kelsey for her if you
didn't get back before dinnertime. I told
her it wasn't a problem."

"That's it?" Paul was beyond the point of
concealing his distress. Despite his insis-
tence a minute ago that everything was fine,
he knew Jamie wasn't fooled. She didn't
need him to spell out that he and Leah were
having problems.

This time Jamie did hesitate. "It wasn't
anything she said, exactly . . ."

"Yes?" he prompted.

"She sounded upset, Paul, as though she'd
been crying. When I asked her about it, she
laughed. But her laugh sounded more like a
sob."

Paul felt wretched. He should never have
left her. If he needed time alone, he could've
mowed the lawn, or cleaned out the garage,
organized his thoughts that way. "You're
positive she didn't give you any indication
of where she was going?"

"I'm sorry, Paul, she didn't. I don't think

she knew herself."

That made sense to Paul. Then again it didn't. Leah was methodical about everything she did. She didn't often act — or react — impulsively. The realization that he'd driven her to this was like a nail through his heart.

"Thanks, Jamie, I appreciate the help."

"I'm sorry I couldn't tell you more."

"You've helped." She'd given him something to hold on to, and Paul needed that.

"If there's anything I can do, call me back, okay?"

"Yes," he said.

"Anything," she reminded him.

They spoke for a few more minutes. Jamie asked if he wanted to talk to Rich, but Paul said no. He was in a rush now, wanting to check the closet. If he could figure out what Leah had taken with her, he might be able to guess where she'd gone.

He practically raced into their bedroom, going through the closet and drawers. Whatever she'd packed, it hadn't been much. The murder mystery that had been on the nightstand was missing. She planned to go someplace and read? That seemed odd.

As far as he could tell, there weren't any clothes missing. Maybe a pair of jeans and a shirt, if that. She hadn't taken her pajamas or her housecoat. Or her toothbrush.

The phone rang just then, and Paul's heart shot into his throat. He hurried into the kitchen and grabbed the receiver, hoping to get it before the ringing woke Kelsey and the twins. They were napping, and Angie had gone home, although she'd promised to come back if he needed her.

"Hello," he said as calmly as he could, although he doubted he was very convincing.

"Paul, it's your father. I'm calling from Montana."

"Dad, hello." Why was his father contacting him? Had he heard from Leah?

"Christy had her baby. A little girl. Six pounds, seven ounces. Cute as can be. She's got lots of dark hair." He paused. "Your mother said she would. Christy had heartburn real bad, and according to Elizabeth, that's a sure sign the baby would have a lot of hair and by heaven, she does."

"That's wonderful, Dad. Another granddaughter."

"They've decided to name her Erin Elizabeth. That has a nice sound, doesn't it? Naturally your mother's pleased — and that's putting it mildly."

"Erin Elizabeth Franklin," Paul repeated.

"Cody's proud as a peacock, as well. He's been handing out cigars to everyone in town. 'Course hardly anyone smokes anymore. Even in a cowboy town like this."

"Congratulate him and Christy for us, won't you?"

"You bet I will," Eric said enthusiastically. "Taylor says to tell you hello. She and Russ are going to be adding to their family again. About time if you ask me, but then no one ever does. Including your mother." He chuckled at his own joke.

"Okay, Dad," Paul said casually, not wanting to alert him to his troubles. "I'll let Jason and Rich know. Do you have any idea when you and Mom will be back in Seattle?"

"Oh, I imagine we'll be back in the next couple of weeks."

"Drive carefully."

"You know I will. Take care, son."

"Thanks, Dad." Paul replaced the receiver. So Christy and Cody were parents now. Despite his current problems, Paul was elated for his sister and brother-in-law. He recalled his own excitement, not so long ago, when Kelsey was born. His joy had soon been dwarfed by concern for Diane, but those precious moments when he'd heard his daughter's first cries would stay in his heart forever.

He sagged into a kitchen chair, knowing there was nothing he could do until he heard from Leah. He could fret and worry, but it wouldn't help. He could list everything he'd done wrong, but that would only depress him further.

Paul was reviewing his conversation with Jamie when the front door opened. Feeling a surge of new hope, he moved out of the kitchen and into the living room. He stopped suddenly as Leah walked inside, suitcase in hand.

She froze when she saw him. Her eyes were red and puffy, her face so pale he wondered if she might be ill. "Hello, Paul," she said softly.

THIRTEEN

"Leah." Paul stepped toward her, then hesitated, as though he was afraid of saying or doing something to intimidate her. "Are you all right?"

She nodded. Tears filled her eyes and her throat, and she hated herself for being so weak. "What about you?"

"I'm fine . . . now that you're home."

His gaze fell to the small suitcase in her hand, and her eyes followed his. She'd forgotten about the bag and was embarrassed now that he'd seen her with it.

Packing her things had been an empty gesture. She'd been distraught, barely aware of what she was doing. All she'd taken was a murder mystery and Ryan's yellow blankie. Maybe the five-year-old didn't need his security blanket, but she sure did.

A book and a blanket! What did she intend to do, curl up under a tree? Spend the rest of her life in hiding?

Even more foolish had been her belief that she could leave Paul and the children, for even one night. They were her breath, her substance, everything that mattered to her.

"I went for a drive," she said, her voice husky with emotion.

"So did I," Paul said, his own voice so deep and rich she could listen to it forever.

"I . . . I thought I should get away for a while . . . clear my head."

"Me, too. I did the same thing."

Courage rose inside her and she took heart, smiling through her tears. "Did you come up with any solutions?"

Paul's eyes held hers steadily. "The same ones that've been staring me in the face for months. What about you?"

"A few."

"Do you want to talk about them?"

Leah nodded. Paul came forward and took the suitcase. "I hope you won't be needing this."

"No . . . I won't be," she whispered as he set it aside.

Then, taking Leah by the hand, he led her to the couch and they both sat down. A small space separated them, but the force of their attraction — no, more than that, their love — seemed to draw them together. Leah shifted closer; so did Paul.

They were silent at first, perhaps afraid of saying the wrong thing, of misunderstanding each other again. It was all Leah could do not to blurt out everything she'd learned, how much she loved Paul and the children. How peace had come to her in a cemetery, standing before her sister's grave.

Paul spoke first. "I went to my brother's," he said.

"Rich?" Leah had talked to Jamie earlier. She'd tried to disguise her unhappiness and done a poor job of it.

"No, Jason. For some unknown reason, I . . . I found myself outside his apartment," he said, staring down at his hands. "I'm glad I went. Jason didn't say much, which meant I did all the talking. Whatever he was thinking, other than to defend you, he kept to himself."

Leah smiled. She didn't know him well, but she'd always liked Jason. He seemed like an overgrown kid, but under the baseball cap was a man with a warm, generous heart.

"So talking helped?" she prodded.

Paul's hands reached for hers. "Yes . . . I realized what a fool I've been."

"We've both been fools."

"When Diane died, I never expected to fall in love again," Paul said. "I didn't think it was possible." He hesitated and looked at her uncertainly. "I don't mean to hurt you by telling you this. . . ."

"You aren't hurting me." She encouraged him with another smile, although emotion was clogging her throat — tears of release and relief.

"I figured a man only finds that kind of love once in his life. Then you came to live with me and the children. In the beginning I was so grateful that I assumed everything I felt for you had to do with appreciation. I owed you so much."

"You never understood that I was the one who had reason to be grateful. It was me —"

"I still have trouble believing that," he said, cutting her off. "You gave up your life for us."

"No, I found it instead. If it hadn't been for you and the children, I would've spent my whole life teaching the quadratic formula and attending faculty meetings. I would've grown old without ever knowing what it means to be in love."

His gaze dropped, as if he had to look away in order to continue. "I don't know if marrying you when I did was the right thing. I was attracted to you. I suspect I was afraid of losing you to Rob Mullins."

"Rob." Leah gave a short laugh. Paul had no idea how much she'd come to dislike her colleague and friend. Former friend. Their last evening together had been a disaster. Rob had tried to pressure her into confessing a sexual relationship with Paul. It seemed beyond his comprehension that the two of them could be living together without sex.

Leah had been insulted and infuriated. She was attracted to Paul and had been for weeks. They'd experienced that one explosive kiss and both had worked hard to avoid repeating it. They'd been constantly aware of each other's proximity. They'd fought their sexual attraction every moment they were together. Some days the tension had seemed intolerable.

So Rob's innuendos had struck a raw nerve. Leah had barely made it through the evening. The poetry reading was nearly two hours north of Seattle, and she'd hardly spoken a word on the long drive back. Rob had tried to fill the silence with questions and snatches of conversation, but she'd met his attempts with one-word replies.

He'd grown impatient with her, and by the time they'd reached Paul's house, he was angry and demanding. Leah had jumped out of his car, said she didn't plan to see him ever again and escaped inside before he could argue or delay her. She hadn't heard from him since, for which she was grateful.

"I was jealous of Rob," Paul was saying. "And I hated myself for it — because it made me aware of several things I wasn't ready to face. First and foremost, I was *feeling* again.

"For months my emotions had been numb. I was desensitized. There were times I laughed, but I was never happy. There were times I looked forward to another day, but I wasn't whole. I wasn't at peace with myself. Six months after Diane's death I was still clinging to her, deathly afraid of what would happen if I ever let her go."

"When your parents suggested we get married, I was stunned." Leah had her own confession to make. "I didn't think you'd want to marry anyone like me. . . ."

"Why not?"

All the old doubts and fears had come back to plague her. All the insecurities of her youth. "I'm not . . . Diane."

"No, you're Leah. Warm, beautiful, gentle Leah."

Leah didn't feel she'd possessed any of those qualities until she'd fallen in love with Paul. "I was afraid."

"But why?" Paul wanted to know, looking bewildered.

"I was convinced that sometime down the road, a year from now, or maybe sooner, you'd wake up and realize you were saddled with me and —"

"*Saddled* with you? Leah —"

"Please, listen." She couldn't allow him to distract her, to keep her from addressing her fears. "I'm not beautiful. I've known it all my life, and I've accepted it." She paused when it looked as though Paul was going to protest again. Pressing her fingers to his lips, she continued, "I don't have a gregarious personality. Or Diane's charm and sense of humor. But I couldn't change who I am, not even to please you. When I agreed to marry you, I did so for purely selfish reasons."

"Leah —"

Once more she stopped him. "I did so because I couldn't bear to leave the children and because . . . because I was falling in love with you, and it scared me to death. I finally had a chance of finding what had always escaped me. A husband, a family, people who loved me, and I grabbed it with both hands."

"Our marriage was unfair to you."

"Don't you understand?" she cried. "*I* was

taking advantage of *you.* I knew the time would come when you'd regret marrying me, yet I went ahead with it anyway."

"Leah, I'm never going to regret marrying you."

"Maybe you should."

"No." He got to his feet and walked to the window, gazing out. "Because, you see, Leah, I discovered I loved you as deeply and profoundly as I've ever loved anyone in my life."

"And I . . . I discovered love through you and the children." Leah's voice was tranquil. Thoughtful. "I discovered what it is and what it means."

Paul turned toward her. "I expected to feel guilty for loving you and I fulfilled that prophecy. Only, to my surprise, I had to force myself to feel the guilt. Anytime I examined my feelings for you, I realized loving you was what Diane would've wanted. But I couldn't admit it, because that would mean letting Diane go, and I wasn't ready to do that.

"I was caught between the two of you. Trapped between the past and the present. The more time I spent with you, the dimmer my vision of Diane became, and that frightened me. Yet I couldn't make myself stop loving you." He looked away from her again.

"Until you thought I might be pregnant . . . Then you couldn't bear to touch me." Leah lowered her eyes because the pain was still there.

"No!" Paul covered the distance between them in three strides. He sat next to her and took her hands in his. "It wasn't that, Leah. It wasn't *anything* like that. I've never known a greater fear than when you told me you might be pregnant. The thought of losing you terrified me. I think I went a little crazy."

He leaned his forehead against hers, and his voice grew rougher. "It was when you thought you might be pregnant that I understood how much I loved you."

Paul's arms came around her then. "I was confronted with my greatest fear. Losing the woman I loved. Now, looking back, I realize how badly I behaved, how much my attitude hurt you. I'm sorry for that, sorrier than you'll ever know."

"You were so angry."

"But never with you. If I blamed anyone, it was myself. At the same time, I recognized how much I loved you — and how much I loved Diane. I didn't know it was possible to love two women so deeply — and then it came to me — I didn't."

Was this what he'd realized when he talked to his brother? Leah wondered. Her heart started to pound louder and louder.

"Friday night . . ."

She pulled her hands free from his and lowered her eyes. Their lovemaking the night before had moved her in a way that went beyond sensual excitement or gratification. Paul had held her in his arms afterward, teased her, laughed with her. He'd made her feel more wanted and loved in one evening than she'd felt in her entire life. She'd gone to sleep content, basking in the joy she'd experienced. A joy that exceeded anything she'd ever hoped to feel.

Then she'd woken to the sound of another woman's name on her husband's lips.

"That night," Paul continued, "was indescribable. Yes, the lovemaking was great, but it always is. You went to sleep in my arms, and as I lay there I realized what was different, what had changed." He tucked his finger under her chin and raised her face until her eyes locked with his. "On Friday night I released Diane. I let go of her and stepped out of yesterday and into today, tomorrow — my life with you."

"But . . . you called me Diane."

"I had a dream," Paul said, his words

heavy with regret. "I can't explain it, but . . . in my dream Diane was there. I can't remember exactly what happened, just bits and pieces of it."

Breathless, Leah stared at him.

"Jason thinks my subconscious had something to do with it," he went on. "He thinks Diane was releasing me, too. I don't know if any of this makes sense to you. But I'm at peace with her death, at peace with myself. It didn't come easy, but . . ." He seemed to be waiting for a reaction from her.

"Diane came to me in a dream once, too," Leah said in a whisper. It was the first time she'd ever told anyone about that experience. "It was the night she died. I was exhausted and I was sure my mind was playing tricks on me. She looked so happy. I couldn't understand it. She was standing under a tree with wildflowers all around her."

"What kind of flowers?"

His question seemed odd to Leah. "I'm not sure, except she was holding a —"

"A daisy."

"Yes." Her eyes widened with surprise. "How'd you know?"

"In my dream she stood under a tree. I remember that much now. She seemed so happy, plucking the petals from a yellow daisy."

"Yes!" Leah flattened her hand over her heart. "Yes," she repeated. "There was a light, too."

"A brilliant light."

Leah nodded again.

"What did she say?" Paul asked her.

"She told me she was going away. I tried to argue with her, tried to make her stay, but she didn't have time to listen to me. She said she'd had to get us away from the hospital because we were holding her back. And then . . . then she explained that she hadn't wanted to go away in the beginning, but had come to understand it would be all right to leave. She . . . she asked me if I'd take her place."

"Take her place?"

Leah nodded. "I didn't understand what she meant, but I didn't question her, either. She looked right at me. I'd never been able to refuse Diane anything, so I promised her I would."

Paul was silent for a moment. "I don't remember what she said to me, but I think Jason might be right. I think she came to say goodbye."

They grew silent, each lost in the memory of the one they'd loved so much.

"It was because of the dream that I eventually decided to live here, in your house, but I never intended to fall in love with you," Leah confessed. "You talked about feeling guilty and being trapped between the past and the present — that's how I felt, too. I was afraid to love you, fighting it, but at the same time I'd never been happier, or more fulfilled."

She didn't know how to put into words everything that was in her heart. How could she explain that she belonged to him in ways she didn't even belong to herself?

"You felt guilty?"

Leah grinned sheepishly. "When I left today, I . . . I went for a drive and ended up at the cemetery. I hadn't been there since the funeral. I wasn't sure where her grave was, and it took me a long time to find it. When I did I just stood there, not knowing what to say, but knowing I had to say something."

"I haven't been there in weeks." Paul's voice was low, incredulous, as if he'd just realized it. "I guess the need to talk to her left me after we got married."

Leah went on. "I told her how well the twins and Kelsey were doing, and then I got angry. I so seldom raise my voice that I think I frightened myself. I hated what was happening to me. Hated competing with her when I'd never wanted to compete before. For the first time in my life, I wanted something she had, and I didn't know how to handle it."

"Oh, Leah . . ." His thumb caressed her cheek. Leah closed her eyes, loving the glorious feel of his skin touching hers.

"I asked her if this was what she wanted — for me to love you. Because it was killing me — loving you, when you loved *her.* I was jealous, and I'd never been before, not once in all the years we grew up together."

Paul pulled her toward him, adjusting their positions so she was cradled in his arms, her head on his chest.

"Did you receive any answers?"

"Yes." She smiled, a smile that radiated out from her heart. "I was standing there, weeping, knowing I was asking the impossible, demanding an answer when there was none to be had. Only . . . there was."

"But how . . . what answer?"

"It'd been raining most of the morning. The sky was dark and overcast."

"Yes," Paul concurred.

"As I was standing there, the sun broke through the clouds. I watched as the sky parted and this brilliant stream of light shot down." Leah wasn't sure whether she should continue, whether Paul would believe her or not. The sun parting the sky wasn't a spectacular miracle; it was an everyday phenomenon. An everyday kind of miracle.

"I had my answer," Leah whispered, close to tears. "You and the children are Diane's gift to me. She gave me what she loved most — you four. She knows me so well. All along she realized I was going to fall in love with you. It's what she wanted."

"She knew I'd love you, too," Paul added. "That we'd both fight it because of our loyalty to her, and yet, if she'd been able, she would've told us our love was by design. Her design."

"She loved us both so much."

"Loves," Paul corrected softly, tightening his embrace. "I don't think that'll ever change." He was still holding her when Leah sensed they were no longer alone.

Slowly she opened her eyes and glanced at the hallway. Ryan stood there, rubbing his eyes. As she watched the child — her child — her heart seemed to expand with all the love she felt.

"Did you sleep well, sweetheart?" she asked.

Ryan nodded. "Kindergartners are too old for naps."

It was a point he argued loudly and often,

and yet he fell asleep of his own accord every afternoon.

"I'm too old for naps, too," Ronnie announced, appearing by his brother's side and yawning widely. "Only babies go to bed in the daytime."

"I'd like to be in bed right now," Paul whispered in Leah's ear. "You wouldn't hear me complaining about taking a nap. If you were taking one with me, that is."

"Paul," she chastised.

"Come here, boys," Paul called his sons. They climbed onto their father's lap as Leah got up to check on Kelsey. If the boys were awake, then their sister probably was, too.

Sure enough, she was standing in her crib, bouncing excitedly. She broke into a grin when she saw Leah.

"How's my darling?" Leah asked. "How's my darling baby girl?"

Kelsey raised her arms to Leah and delivered a sentence or two of happy gibberish.

Leah and Kelsey joined Paul and the boys, and the five of them sat together on the sofa — Paul holding the twins and Leah holding Kelsey. The five of them were truly a family, Leah realized. One formed in love. A gift she'd received from her sister.

Paul's eyes met hers and he smiled.

Leah smiled, too. She felt his love — in

his smile, his touch, the warm look in his eyes.

Love . . . It was more than she'd ever dared to dream. More than she'd ever thought to have.

Love had found a place for her.

We hope you have enjoyed this Large Print book. Other Thorndike, Wheeler, Kennebec, and Chivers Press Large Print books are available at your library or directly from the publishers.

For information about current and upcoming titles, please call or write, without obligation, to:

Publisher
Thorndike Press
295 Kennedy Memorial Drive
Waterville, ME 04901
Tel. (800) 223-1244

or visit our Web site at:

http://gale.cengage.com/thorndike

OR

Chivers Large Print
published by BBC Audiobooks Ltd
St James House, The Square
Lower Bristol Road
Bath BA2 3SB
England
Tel. +44(0) 800 136919
email: bbcaudiobooks@bbc.co.uk
www.bbcaudiobooks.co.uk

All our Large Print titles are designed for easy reading, and all our books are made to last.